Red Horizon

By
Jason R. LaPoint

Red Horizon Dedications:

The Pitch for Dan Foster..................................p.12
Cars for Charyl Natale....................................p.33
Little Fish for Zac LaPoint..............................p.81
Leviatos for Alex Hyatt.................................p.107
Lady of the Wall for Charity Anderson..............p.139
OR-B for Patti LaPoint................................p.180
The Tenacious Nature of Bees for David Haviland...p.192
Last Goodbye for Jessica LaPoint p.223

Red Horizon
Prologue

I grew up watching stuff like Star Search and I think that has a lot to do with my skewed world perspective. In my early life I was every bit a product of 80's cultural brainwashing. I thought rattails were cool. I even liked Warrant for a minute. In short I was a mess just like most of my generation. But, the first time I discovered Charles Bukowski that perspective changed forever. I read the poems, I saw the pictures and I thought, wait, you can be a successful artist and still not care what people think about you? It was by learning about him that I came to understand that some people still value their perception of the art over their perception of the artist. In short Chuck B. indirectly taught me that image is not everything but rather honest expression of your vision is. This concept flew in the face of all that Star Search had taught me before. This realization blew my fragile eggshell mind and from then on I felt free to write whatever I wanted to. It was liberating. It opened up a whole new world of experiences for me in reading, writing and life in general. Some of those experiences were good and some of them were bad. But all of them were necessary steps of the road I am on. And what a road it has been.

You can't really know yourself until you wake up hung over in an apartment you don't recognize with a whiskey stained paper back of "To Have and Have Not" stuck to your face. Those nights, or rather those mornings made me who I am today. My twenties were filled with them. The nights are easy to romanticize but the mornings are stark reality. The mornings are when the walk of shame happens. The mornings are when I write best.

For me the essence of real art lies in taking things

right to the edge of control, to the edge of sanity even, and then seeing how far over the line you can go and still make it back. Some make it back and some don't. Luckily for me I did, or at least I think I did. But those who never push the limits never truly live at all. There is a part in "Gimme Shelter" where Merry Clayton is soul singing. If you listen close right near the end of her solo, for a brief moment her voice breaks into a scream. She loses control ever so slightly for just a heartbeat and every time I hear that it gives me chills. Merry gets it, she understands. That is definitely not a Star Search moment. There is no fluff in that moment.

The instant where singing and screaming meet, that is it. That is the edge. That is where a real artist, a brave artist has to live. On the edge there is no room for the timid. The edge is life with the stark reality of morning. It is where all of the sins are exposed and on display. I hate the edge and I love it at the same time. I need it. The world needs it.

Beyond the edge lies the red horizon. In the beginning my red horizon was inspired by a Jeff Buckley quote that resonated with me for reasons I honestly can't recall. In one of his songs he uses the image of a flaming red horizon as a metaphor for death. He is making a point about the frivolous machinations of the world's power mongers since in spite of their efforts at controlling us, the world and each other; death awaits us all including them. In the beginning I think I just dug the mental scene the lyric painted. I had this Dantean image of Washington politicians and greedy corporate CEOs pooping their pants as some unseen force conveyed them into a fiery sunset to face their due judgment.

But the concept of the red horizon has evolved in my mind over time into something more. When I started writing this book I was very young. I was a naïve man and a naïve artist. I knew enough to appreciate poetry like Jeff's but not enough to really understand it. I started writing the earliest stories in this book nearly twelve years ago and finished them only recently. For a long time I thought not finishing these pieces faster was due to some fault of mine. But now I no longer believe that. I think the universe, the gods, the ghost of Charles Bukowski, or whatever the hell runs all of this, was making me wait.

I had talent in the beginning but I wasn't ready yet to say what needed to be said. For one thing I was soft in the backbone in the early days. It's sad to admit that but I have to call it like it is. I had to face some tests and I had to atone for some sins. For another thing I was still pretty closed minded. That was mostly because I had a pretty sheltered childhood and I hadn't had any mind bending experiences yet. Any real pain I'd faced up to that point had been self-inflicted and that kind of pain doesn't count on the path to enlightenment my friends.

In effect I was a 25 year old little boy who'd spent his whole life running from the very pain I felt compelled to use as the subject of my art. I had to stop being scared and the only way to do that is to face what scares you. The only people who aren't afraid of hell are those of us who have already been there. In short I had to wake up and quite frankly I had to learn to write. The ghost of Charles Bukowski and God were slowing me down so I wouldn't go out and make a big ass of my self because trust me the early drafts of some of these stories were about as far from art as you can get. They weren't brave and they weren't well written but there was something about them; something that I couldn't give up on. That's why even after a decade of changes in my life and changes in who I've become as a writer; I kept coming back to them until they were done.

As I evolved, Red Horizon also evolved. It evolved from a cautionary tale in a song into a promise for me.

Because I do understand what Jeff was singing about now and it no longer scares me. I don't fear the pain of life or death any more. But more importantly I don't fear the power mongers any more and that is how I know I'm ready. Because if you fear them you can't challenge them and I am the type of artist who has to challenge them otherwise my art is an impotent paint by numbers kit.

There is an under-current in all of these stories. They all suggest that there is something menacing which flows through the world as I see it. The supernatural boogie-men who appear in a few of these tales are nothing compared to this larger evil. This thinly veiled darkness permeates everywhere in our world and it is all too real. But you can not fear it. Your fear is just what it wants. The power mongers spread the fear with "terror threats" and 24 hour news cycles filled with shootings and riots. They tell lies about other cultures; they tell you how jealous the world is of us, and they tell you they are only out to protect you. In truth they are only out to survive and for a thing to survive a thing must feed and what this thing feeds on is your fear. Don't feed it. The red horizon waits whether you fear it or not. The unknown is inescapable and *it* holds the real power not these other people. Don't fear the horizon and don't fear men. Face them both. Men only hold power over one another in this realm. And the truth about the horizon is that it really is nothing to fear at all.

It is where the singing becomes a scream. It is the edge. It is where I live when I sit down at this computer. It is that edge that I feel my stories have, the edge that they lacked when I started this journey. But now that I have seen that red horizon instead of just hearing Jeff sing about it I feel ready to go forward. I feel like I am ready to tell my story. All of the things that I have learned from Charles Bukowski, Jeff Buckley and Merry Clayton have made me ready. I now understand that the Star Search mentality has no place where I'm going. Art is not a golden ticket to wealth or fame. It is about trying to honestly express these visions that are constantly beaming into my head from that burning place beyond the sunset.

It is by realizing this truth and giving up my quest for the golden nightmare that I became free. This ride I'm on isn't laden with greed or fear any longer. Now I am free to hit the road and attempt to turn all of my crazy into something beautiful. Come along for the ride if you'd like, but I'm going with or without you. I know where this all ends and what the road will be like. It is long and broken and there are no exits. There is just the red horizon ever lying ahead.

Jason
11-23-13, 21:09
Thurman, NY

The Pitch

I have been doing this for years. Every morning I wake up promptly at 5:45 to the sound of Skipper Donovan's gravelly voice as he delivers the WFOS sports report. "Last night, in front of *another* sell out crowd, the Sox put a shellacking on the Minnesota Twins at Fenway Park, thanks to two homeruns by Big Papi and an eight inning, two hit performance by Timmy Wakefield. Foulke closed it out in the ninth capping off the shutout before the ecstatic Fenway crowd. That's sports on WFOS, Fan of Sox!"

I generally hit the snooze button right about there and fall back to sleep for nine more minutes. Sometimes I simply lay staring at the ceiling for awhile and reflect on how Skipper is probably the only person in the world who calls Wakefield "Timmy". But eventually the snooze time runs out and the rolling bass of Radar Love or the haunting melody of Gold Dust Woman gently prod me into reality.

Slowly I drag myself out of bed and into the shower, squinting against the glare of the bathroom lights. The warm water massages away the last remnants of sleep and as my mind comes alive I begin to plan the day's work.

Which route I should canvass is always my first consideration. The route is the story's setting, the play's stage, the movie's set, whatever metaphor you like; it is where the pitch really begins. The route is in fact more important to the success of the pitch than the pitch itself. No matter if I succeed or fail it is the route that allows the pitch to happen in the first place.

On this particular day the route was a beauty indeed, but not because prime customers lived on it or because it was in a wealthy part of town. Although both of those things were true neither of them matter very much. The route was a beauty quite simply because it is in a wooded, shady section of Kenyon Mills. One of Skipper Donovan's cohorts, Mike "the Weatherguy" Murphy told the WFOS faithful this morning that today's high temperature would be in the high nineties and may even reach one hundred degrees. Temperatures like that are detrimental to a well delivered pitch. Folks are already apprehensive when a stranger darkens their doorstep. If the stranger is pasty skinned and dripping with sweat they are even less likely to let him in. One must have a pleasant appearance if one wishes to be successful in this business. If my kind had a set of commandments that would very likely be one of the first ones. The shade would certainly be a welcome thing.

  I left the house at 6:30. I stopped at Cobble Stone Farms for coffee and gas and then it was off to the route to earn my daily bread. I drove through Kenyon Mills enjoying the bucolic charm of the town. It is always so quiet that early in the morning, before the horns and revving engines and squawking townsfolk come out and ruin everything. As I cruised I had a sudden overwhelming sense of joy, like people sometimes do, for no particular reason. I don't really know how to describe that feeling, I just suddenly felt young. The feeling washed over me like the water in a pool on a hot day. I drove with the early morning sun on my face and I could actually palpate my own youth and it occurred to me that I wouldn't always have it. I wouldn't always be able to dance to a song on the radio or hold my bladder until the next rest stop. But at that moment the realization of my inevitable dotage was a non factor. All of that frailty hadn't yet arrived in me and my awareness that it was coming couldn't change the fact that right at that moment I felt great. I was young, healthy and alive more so than I ever had been. This epiphany came out of nowhere like an afternoon breeze.

I pulled my car into the parking lot by the little league field on Chestnut St. It was nearly seven and the morning fog had burnt off almost completely. I pulled a cigarette from the inside pocket of my suit jacket and touched the glowing coil of the car lighter to the tip. I exhaled the first drag of the day, took a sip of coffee and opened my briefcase which always rides in the passenger seat beside me. I took out my list of names and a small stack of contract forms. The first name on the list was Stutzman, Anna and Fredrick. The little bio beside it read:

>Stutzman, Anna A. and Fredrick P.
>14 Chestnut St, Kenyon Mills, NY
>HW- W/L H/D – CNW 535K

The cryptic bio is really just basic shorthand. The address and name are obvious. The third line simply reads:

Husband and wife, wife living, husband deceased, combined net worth five hundred thirty five thousand dollars. Pretty informative wouldn't you say?

"Grab that cash with both hands and make a stash," I said to myself as I exhaled another drag of smoke.

One piece of information not on the bio, however vitally important to the pitch, is her religious affiliation. It's not on the bio because it doesn't have to be. All of my customers are Christians. It doesn't matter which denomination they subscribe to so long as they are a good living, lake of fire fearing, Jesus Man follower. This factor is why I choose towns like Kenyon Mills in the first place. It isn't the high per capita income it is the utter lack of religious diversity in these white-bread, upstate New York towns. There are other religious inclinations here but they are a minority. Truth is you can't swing a numb-chuck without hitting a Methodists or a Catholic around here. And that's just the way I like it. Those are my people.

I stuffed the papers back into my briefcase and headed north up Chestnut St. on foot with my coffee in one hand and the briefcase in the other. As I climbed the front steps of the Stutzman residence I noticed that the front door was open and only the screen door stood between me and the interior of the house. I smiled.

"One small barrier for me, one giant leap for Anna Stutzman," I thought as I rang the doorbell.

The smell of potpourri wafted out of the house. It smelled like peaches and cat piss. Charming. I could hear the quacking of the talking heads on the Today show coming from the living room along with Anna's gentle footfalls. I was straightening my tie as she approached the screen door. She had the same half skeptical, half intrigued look that almost every customer I've ever met has worn on their face. She had short white hair that was curled- artificially of course- and a blue house coat that was positively spackled with printed flowers. A big smile rose on her face that caused her horn rimmed schoolmarm glasses to ride up high on the bridge of her nose.

"Hello, can I help you?" She said as she unlatched the screen door.

My smile widened as the latch dropped and she swung the door open without so much as a word from me. Too easy, sometimes it's just too damned easy.

"Good Morning, Mrs...," I put in a nice scripted pause as I looked at the clipboard fastened to the front of my briefcase. As if I didn't already know her name and every other relevant thing about her. "...Stutzman. How are you this fine morning?"

"Very well, thank you," she said and smiled, pulling the lapels of her house coat together and stretching to see what was written on the clipboard from which I had so mysteriously pulled her name.

"My name is Alan Nikolski. I represent Bristol Mission Services and I wonder if I could have a few minutes of your time?"

If she said yes to this question she was giving me permission to sell her. It is the first yes in a paver brick pathway of yeses.

I leaned subtly toward the open doorway. Body language is the key to using the power of suggestion to its fullest potential. She paused apprehensively and looked around me first left then right down the street.

"Where is your car?" She asked.

"Oh I'm on foot. I'm speaking to everyone I can and it seems such a waste to drive a car only to stop at every house I pass." Then I paused again and looked out at the lawn and the street beyond. The sun was already bright. It really was going to be a cooker today. "I wonder if I couldn't come in. I'll only be a minute and even if you aren't interested in what I have to say at least you'll be getting me out of the heat for a few minutes. What do you say?"

This is just more of the pitch. I am playing on the love thy neighbor, Good Samaritan thing. You can see how the Crucifixians are my best targets. If they are good little bible thumpers they can't help themselves.

Anna thought for a moment and looked me up and down. I gave her my best former-altar-boy smile then finally she said, "Sure, Mr. Noloskin, Nibroski…" Then she pushed the screen door open the rest of the way and let me in; my first yes. She was mine.

"Nikolski, ma'am but that's alright, you can call me Alan," I said. Then I showed a big toothy smile that little old ladies almost never conceive of as being devilish. But it is, it definitely is.

"Alright, Alan, take a seat on the sofa and I will be right with you."

"Sofa," I thought to myself, this is a done deal.

I sat on the sofa and she went to the kitchen. She called back over her shoulder, "Would you like some Kona, Mr.…uh…Alan?"

"Yes ma'am I sure would," I replied.

No matter what they offer whether it is food, drinks, dirty jokes, whatever, a good salesman always accepts the gift happily and even if it's the worst food, coffee or joke in the world he will eat, drink or laugh like it was the best.

"Kona" she said, not just coffee or Maxwell House or Hills Brothers, but Kona. Fancy imported coffee was about the only extravagance evident in the house. Family pictures covered the walls not art. Shag carpet covered the floor not parquet. A twenty inch TV sat in the corner of the living room with the rabbit ear/tin foil antenna combo and I was actually surprised to see Katie Couric's face in color instead of black and white. The money had to be in stocks or cash savings because this house wasn't worth anywhere close to 500K. If you sold it and everything in it at auction you'd be lucky to pull in a quarter of that. But it made no difference to me. Not every score had to be the Brink's Job. I could absorb three or four of these small takes per month without starving, trust me.

Anna came back into the room with a small silver tray which held a porcelain urn, two porcelain cups with saucers and two small bowls. One of the bowls was filled with sugar packets and the other held several single serving creamer cups like the ones used in diners. She first filled my cup and then hers; the perfect hostess. When she finished she sat in the chair across from me and folded her hands in her lap. Then she waited patiently for the inevitable; the pitch. A small oak coffee table was all that separated the spider from the fly.

"I didn't know how you took it so I brought you everything. Myself, I like it black," Anna said after watching me silently for a moment and waiting.

I smiled tacitly and fixed my coffee prolonging the silence for a minute more. The patient use of silence is one of the oldest tricks in the book. The customer knows you are going to sell them something but they don't yet know what or how you will do it. A few moments of anticipation can pique their interest. But, too much can have the reverse effect. It's almost like dead air on your favorite radio station between songs. For a few seconds you wait in anticipation, you can almost see the DJ picking your favorite CD off of the shelf and queuing it up. But, if the dead air lasts too long one's patience wears out and channel surfing ensues.

I finished preparing the coffee, two creams, two sugars, the same way my father always took it. I brushed my hands together, took a sip and then placed the cup gently back on the saucer. Kona really is incredible. Then I looked Anna in the eyes solemnly and began.

"Anna, do you believe in heaven?"

This is a bold, attention grabbing question to be sure, especially coming from a complete stranger at seven in the morning. Whatever my clients are expecting when I enter their home it isn't anything that begins with this question. Of that I am quite certain. But I do so love misdirection and the element of surprise. I know just how the cat feels as he bats a mouse around simply for the visceral pleasure of it.

For a moment she just looked at me, like they always do, then she said almost shyly but with conviction, "Well, yes, yes I do!"

Then I said, "Do you believe you are going there?"

Ooh, I can almost feel her shock setting in, can't you? She is thinking something along the lines of "who the hell are you? What do you want from me? Get out of my house." But she's just too damned well trained to say any of that. She's been taught her whole life to be patient and to turn the other cheek and all of that dribble. Oh, how I love that dribble so! Instead of getting angry with me she sits there with her rheumy eyes growing even wetter trying to figure out my angle. Then I turned up the heat.

I said, "More importantly do you believe Frederick went there?"

It is all part of the trick of course. With the younger more desensitized generations the pitch couldn't work. But, shock value still has an impact on these Rosie the Riveter era gals. It's a well planned and well practiced script, that I make seem so spontaneous. To Anna, it's a shocking conversation, as shocking as the proposition that follows it, almost. To me it's as shocking as a rerun TV show. The trick is to add fuel to that ever smoldering fire in the mind called self doubt. "Do you believe you are going there?" Pause. It's such, an amazingly powerful septet of words in this context no matter the belief system of the recipient of the question. But it works best on the Christians. Even more specifically the Catholics, they buy it the most. It isn't so much true of the "born again" type. They have a sort of religious arrogance. But the lifers are just filled with guilt. From the time a Catholic is old enough to understand the concept of God they are programmed to think they are unworthy of Him. The Catholic principle of faith based on guilt and shame is what makes the pitch work so well. It is why I always pick Christians and it is also why the pitch almost never fails.

Again Anna could have gotten angry and tried to throw me out at this point, some customers do. But she didn't, instead she just looked past me out the window for a moment. I could almost see her thoughts, the things she'd done in her life that her faith had made her regret; normal, human things, things which are unworthy of a moment's shame. Evenings of back seat barnstorming as a teenager, a few too many Tom Collins at bridge club, fibbing about this or flubbing up that. To a Catholic it doesn't matter how minor the sin is it stays with them forever. It burrows into their soul like a termite and finds a spot down in the depths behind the shelves where the old memories are stored away and it smolders, like the cherry of a cigarette dropped into the crack of a recliner chair. It sits and smolders just waiting for the right temperature or a gust of fresh air to ignite it into an all consuming inferno. I and my pitch are that gust of air. And what ever she may have been recalling, however unfounded her guilt over those things may have been it was all part of the pitch. But, I knew that while all of this was true, it was really more the question of Frederick's fidelity than hers which was eating at her. Was he in heaven? She didn't know. What had he done that she didn't know about? They'd been married forty-seven years when he died. That's a long time. There were a lot of business trips and Lodge meetings in all that time. Had he done anything in her absence to condemn his mortal soul? She just couldn't be sure and it had been digging at her since long before Alan Nikolski came along. But now I had come along and I had unearthed her greatest fear. I am a smooth criminal.

    I let her stew in her own juices for what felt like a decent amount of time. Then when I thought she was sufficiently unsure of herself and her husband I went for the jugular.

I said, "How would you like to be able to answer yes to both of those questions, Anna? How would you like to know for sure, beyond any doubt at all that you and Frederick will rest in peace together forever?"

By now any sane person would have asked, "Who are you?" or "What are you selling?" But Anna didn't, she couldn't and she wasn't sane, not right at that moment anyway. That flame of regret had stoked up now and the smoke and heat of it were clouding her mind. That is how it works. If I deliver it right, like I did with Anna, if all of the elements fall into place, it always works. Why wouldn't it? Who wouldn't want a little redemption insurance? Who wouldn't want to know for sure that they were taking the great glass elevator to the penthouse instead of the basement? The pitch gives them what they most desire, even now at this stage; not knowing what I was talking about, only knowing that she had to be able to answer yes, for herself as much as for her dead husband. It wasn't just that I wanted her to say yes it was that she needed to say it.

"I would like to say yes, oh God I would. I am so sorry for everything," she said. Then she broke down and began to sob. I began to smile.

"There is no need to be sorry, Anna. Not to me, I am no priest. I'm just a pardoner, in a manner of speaking. I'm just a regular guy who knows a few tricks in this arena. Those tricks are something I can use to give you the ability to say yes to my question with all confidence," I said.

When she turned her confused eyes back to me I looked for a flicker of doubt but there was none. She had no idea what I was talking about but it was beyond certain that she was all in so far.

I went on, "I can give you the power to say, 'Yes, I am going to heaven, yes I am sure, I am saved, I have atoned and I am sanctified!'"

I was on a roll now, like Jerry Falwell on the Old Time Gospel Hour. And my studio audience, Anna, was on the edge of her seat, coming out of the depths of her woe one step at a time with my every word, leaning forward waiting to be biffed on the forehead so all of her demons could be knocked out of her sinful soul.

I gave another scripted pause. The Today show babbled in the background, cars zipped by on Chestnut St. and just like the weather outside, in the Stutzman living room I was getting hot. I could feel it. I could see it in her eyes. Anna was almost smiling now, her eyes which were wet with regret moments ago were now wet with hope and she hung on my every word, yearning to know how I could give her what seventy-seven years of blind faith and constant prayer could not. How could I, a traveling salesman, albeit a strange one for sure, give her the peace of mind that her religion could not?

And then it came. It was what I had been waiting for. It was the key, the overtime touchdown pass; the head cheerleader spreading her legs on prom night, the white flag of surrender.

"How can you do that?" She almost whispered it.

She looked at me with a face that poker pros dream of. The look on her face told me unequivocally that the deal was done. She may as well have grabbed my pen and a contract form and started writing. But, it isn't quite that easy. I had one more bridge to cross. It was delicate but if I was careful this one was mine. Yes, she was so close it was mine to lose. Just one more step, the fat lady singing, the point after kick…

"By letting me *buy* your sins," I said. Then I folded my hands and leaned back on the sofa. I let my eyes fall to my lap briefly and then raised them back up to hers and waited.

Now I'm not saying that any of the pitch is in the realm of normal conversation, but this last proposition is bizarre even compared to the oddity of all that came before it. But strange as it may be that proposition is the essence of the pitch. It is the thing that all of this hinges on. In fact my very existence hinges on it. I know that it takes an enormous leap of faith for anyone to listen beyond this particular reveal. But, I need them to listen. So all I can do is have faith that I have prepared them properly going into it and then hope for the best. Patience is my cutlass from this point on. I have to be like Papi sitting on a low hanging curveball; patience, timing, wait.

"Buy…my…sins? I don't follow?" Anna said puzzled.

The pitch's twist, the big switcharooski, the thing that makes it so sweet is that it isn't a sale at all, it's actually a purchase. They never see it coming. It knocks them for a loop every time.

"Anna, have you ever heard of a Sin-eater?" I asked, leaning forward and looking strait into her eyes.

"No," she said sounding like a little kid who has just been accused of stealing a cookie.

"There are a few different versions of the legend, the most common one tells us the sin-eaters come to the home of a recently deceased person and consume everything in their home, thereby consuming; or rather assuming the newly deceased person's sins. The truth of the matter is that most of the sin-eaters of legend were frauds. They were looking for a free meal and they got it by preying on the bereaving families of the recently deceased. All they really did was trick the poor people into giving away their inheritance. But, I and my ancestors are true sin-eaters and after many generations we have found a way to overcome the stigma that these avaricious imposters have cast upon our kind. We are legitimate sin-eaters called Ouaske. We have been around for millennia. We canvass the earth seeking out hell-bound souls. We purchase your vessels of sin at a very handsome price before you die and when that day comes we come back to hold up our end of the deal."

    She was clearly at sea so I let her think it over in silence for awhile. After a few minutes I pulled out my pen and a contract and laid them on the table in front of her. Doing this invariably triggers a response from my clients but more importantly it answers questions for me. Depending on their reaction to seeing the contract I can usually tell whether or not I've succeeded with the pitch. If they ask me questions I usually have a shot but if I am going to get the door slammed on me this is almost always the point when it happens.

"Well what do you pay, what are the terms?" Anna asked.

Just as she'd done since I first arrived on her porch she left the door wide open. So as I answered her I slid the contract across the table a little closer to her. The power of suggestion is strong with the hot ones.

"The terms are really quite simple. I pay you one million dollars and you sign over all of your vessels of sin to be obtained by me upon your death. You get the money today and you can have peace of mind for the rest of your life knowing that you will in fact be welcomed into God's heaven when the time comes."

At this point of the game, there really is no more game. What ever she asks me from here on I answer her. If she wants facts, I give her facts and the more questions she asks the better, because if she is talking, she isn't reading.

I handed her the pen and showed her where to sign. She glanced at the contract, which was filled with confusing and vague jargon that she didn't understand. I knew she didn't understand it, just as her car salesman, doctor, lawyer and insurance agents all knew that she didn't understand their paperwork either. And just like them I "explained" it to her. And also just like them that means I paraphrased and erred and omitted my way through it telling her what she wanted to hear simply to manipulate her into doing what I wanted her to do.

"See here Anna, its simple; it says I Alan Nikolski, of Bristol Mission Service pay Anna Stutzman the sum of one million dollars for all of her vessels of sin. All you have to do is sign right...um- as if I didn't know where, *I know ma'am these things are just so darn confusing, gosh, I'm just like you that must be why you trust me sooo much.-* here."

Anna looked me in the eyes and hesitated for just a moment then she took the pen and reached for the contract. Just as the pen was about to touch the paper I took her hand and said, "You know that this works for Fred too. This stuff was every bit as much his as it is yours."

A tear formed in the corner of her eye and when her smile made its way that far north the tear rolled down her cheek. Then she actually reached over the table and hugged me. If there were a hell I'd surely be on my way. It's a good thing there isn't. She nodded and eagerly signed my contract and as she did I just couldn't help but grin.

Six months later, the day after she died, I was at the estate auction selling off her "vessels of sin" which in the Definitions section of the contract is explained as "all worldly possessions" (That incidentally includes whatever she might have left from the million that Bristol Mission paid her) when my lawyer called to tell me that the judge had found in my favor. Her son tried to sue me over the contract like they all do but as always the deal was air tight.

As I hung up the phone a white porcelain tea set came up on auction block. A woman in a pink sundress raised her paddle and won the bidding at two hundred dollars and I couldn't help but smile. It's not really a scam you see. They try to call me a con artist. They say I take advantage of the elderly. They say all kinds of nasty things. But the truth is she got what I promised. She died knowing in her heart she was going to heaven with Fred. And besides, a guy's got to make a living.

Jason R. LaPoint
September 2005
Clifton Park, NY

Cars:
The Ghost in the Machine

Albert Jr. sat by the big oriel window looking somberly out at the world. He looked like a little boy sitting in the large dimly lit sitting room alone though he was a full grown man. He was shrunken; shrunken by his grief and his overall station in life. He hadn't said a word all day which was normal for him unless I was around. Albert Jr. never talked to anyone else but when I was there with him his mouth ran like a whippoorwill's ass. His favorite subjects were baseball, women and of course cars.

Albert was fascinated by cars. He read magazines about them, he watched television shows about them and he watched the real thing through his big picture-window all day everyday as they cruised eternally up and down the street.

On a normal day one would catch his eye every so often and he'd shout out to me excitedly, "Ray, Ray, did you see that Beemer? I love the lines on those fucking things. Sleeker than shit man, sleeker than shit."

It was always the same, foul mouthed and enthusiastic, Albert Jr. would give a running commentary on the traffic that passed below his city window, but not today. Today was no normal day and Albert Jr. was not in a normal mood. Under the circumstances I could understand, it isn't every day that a man has to bury his father.

I sat at the dining room table silently watching him for awhile. Every so often he cuffed the sleeve of his shirt over his hand and wiped the condensation from his breath off the window. Then he'd run the sleeve over his face to brush away some tears and resume his gaze through the rain streaked glass. I have heard that rain on the day of a funeral is good luck. Or maybe it was weddings? I honestly never had any use for luck so I wouldn't know.

After a time I stubbed out my cigarette and walked

over to where he sat. I stood behind him for awhile and listened to the cars hiss by on the rainy street outside. There were crumbs mashed into the edges of his seat cushion and his control panel was smeared with something greasy. I made a mental note to clean up his wheelchair before the service. I'd have to do it during his morning nap. Nap time was the only time he would get out of the chair. He thought himself pathetic if he lost his freedom of movement for any length of time. I never thought he was pathetic but if the roles were reversed I guess I could understand. I saw no shame in Al Jr. being confined to a wheelchair, but I couldn't abide him being confined to a filthy one, not on my watch.

I reached out and touched his shoulder. "Come on Al, you have to lie down for awhile before the service. We have a long day ahead of us."

"Fuck you, Ray," he said. There was no bite to his words though. It was an impotent insult. Albert Jr. loves me like a brother and he never gets angry with me. All his other caregivers are a different story. But me, I'm his pal.

"Come on," I said softly and patted his shoulder again.

This time he pouted but he didn't protest. He

thumbed the power button on the chair and deftly spun it around. He whirred away through the sitting room and disappeared down the hall.

I felt bad for the guy for so many reasons beyond just the loss of his dad. I truly pitied him and pity isn't really in my nature. I've seen way too much suffering to be given to pity. My own life has been blessed. Every stupid thing I've done I have escaped barely bruised but my patients are a different story. Most people don't have a clue what real pain is. I have seen patients in renal failure who spend so much time at dialysis they receive their mail at the hospital. I have seen all manner of death and disease. I have watched newly wed wives cry over the death bed of a cancer stricken husband. I have seen the elderly confined to a "rest home" because there is literally no one left alive who can take care of them. I could go on and on but I won't bore you with my observations of misery. I'm sure you have plenty of your own. Suffice it to say that I'm not much for feeling sorry for people. I feel differently about Albert Jr. however. But I pity him more for his regret than for his physical suffering. Regret is something I can understand all too well.

Albert was trying to get into bed alone when I

entered his room. He knew that was against the rules but he was clearly in a defiant mood today. I didn't let him get to me. I knew he was trying to get me mad so he would have a reason to blow his top and let out some of that angry energy he was harboring. But I wasn't going to let him have that. He could yell at Meg the night nurse. I was in no mood for bullshit. What he was forgetting in his state of mourning was that I was also close to his dad and so I was also in mourning. But it isn't Al's job to worry about my feelings, so I simply helped him into bed without a word about his minor rebellion.

"You rest Al. I'm going to clean this chair up like new and get your suit ready for later, cool?"

He didn't answer he just stared at the ceiling.

"After the service we'll come home and watch the Rays and have a brew, what do you say?"

He still didn't answer but the pout faded and I could see his wheels turning in a different direction. He'd be alright once the unpleasant business was behind him. Albert couldn't stay mad at me for long even on a day like this one. I'd get him through the funeral then we'd come home and look through some old pictures of Al Sr. and watch the ball game. By bedtime we'd be on the road to whatever our new normal was going to be.

I left Albert Jr. to rest and wheeled the chair out to the garage. There is no off feature whereby you can just push it like a normal wheelchair so I had to drive it by the joy stick while bending over the chair and clumsily guiding it all the way through the house. I felt like an idiot, this is not a chore that can be accomplished with any grace. But I finally got it to the garage without marking up the walls or breaking anything.

I parked the chair in the center of the empty garage and cooled my head for awhile. This would be the only me time of the day. I would have to be Albert Jr.'s aide all day but for the next two hours or so I could deal with my own grief in peace. The mindless chore of cleaning the chair would be the perfect therapy. My hands could work on the task leaving my mind free to roam.

I cleaned the chair for the next hour and a half until it was beyond spotless, tears streamed down my face the entire time. Albert Sr. was nothing short of a hero to me it's that simple. My respect for him was the main reason I started taking care of his son in the first place. Al Jr. and I shared that respect for his dad and that is what made us such good friends. Over time we've grown close as we've gotten to know each other. But in the beginning, the initial icebreaker was our mutual admiration for his father. I think that is one of the reasons he has always treated me so much different than his other aides. None of them bothered to take the time to understand Al's dad like I did and to him that was unfathomable. Since I know Albert Sr.'s story I can understand full well why Al feels that way.

Albert Sr. was my patient first, that's where it all started. I first met him early in my career when I was an orderly at St Francis Hospital in Arkham Falls. I used to work the 3-11 shift transporting patients to the various parts of the hospital for tests and what have you. I wasn't an integral part of the care giving team in any strict sense but I'm very sociable and many people used to tell me that their ten minute conversation with me on the way to have a CT scan was the most enjoyable part of their day. They felt comfortable talking to someone about anything other than what they were hospitalized for. I was something akin to a reality break for most of them and that was how I always tried to approach my job.

It was during such a trip that Albert Sr. and I first hit it off. I was sent to get him for some test or other and when I arrived in his room he was watching a ballgame on television. I told him it was time to go for his test and he told me to have a seat and wait five minutes because Miguel Cabrera was at bat and the test could wait. Most hospital people aren't very open-minded about doing things on the patient's schedule. Its always rush, rush, rush, we have to get this done now. And usually the rush has nothing to do with the patient; in truth most of the time it is so the worker can get to break or the time clock faster, I'm sad to admit that but it is what it is. But I was never the type to act that way as I said what I do isn't integral. There is no need for urgency. My patient's comfort and happiness is more important to me than anything else. So, I sat down on the foot of his bed and watched Barry Zito pitch to Miguel Cabrera.

    This was in the pre-Tiger days for Miggy. He was still a Marlin back then and he was a lanky fresh faced version of the perennial MVP we've come to know. Zito went up on him 0-2 and I started to go for the wheel chair. Albert Sr. silently held his hand out, indicating that I should wait. He never took his eyes off the screen. So I sat back down.

    Zito walked around the mound and adjusted his cap. Then he went to the rubber, dug in and looked in for the sign. Benji Molina was catching for the Giants. Molina put down a fist and stabbed his pinky to the side.

Zito nodded and went into his motion. He reached back and heaved a monster curve that started high. Benji set up outside where he'd wanted the curve ball to end up; a classic paint the corner strike out pitch. The trouble is it never dropped. The ball stayed high and slow right over the meaty part of the plate and even a nubile Miggy knew a gift when he saw it. He cocked back and teed off on the pitch like it was a whiffle ball. Benji just dropped his head. Zito watched the ball fly over his head and most of the bleachers like a missile then he spit in the dirt and called for a new ball as Miggy trotted around the bags.

"I thought Barry had him," I said.

"Never count that kid out. I'm telling you he's gonna be a great one," Albert Sr. said.

"You think so?"

"I know so."

I helped him to the chair and as we wove through the halls of St Francis we talked non stop about Miggy, Zito and a hundred other things baseball. He was in the hospital for a few months, I forget why but it may have been early trouble with the cancer that would end up putting him in the ground. But that was still a few years off. Over his time at St Francis I saw him almost daily and every time I did the topic invariably turned to baseball. I live for the game and so did he. Baseball nuts are funny critters, we always seem to find our own.

One night before my shift I stopped in to say hi. I'd started doing that once a week or so with him. Some patients just strike a chord with me and he was one of them. That night was the first night of the MLB playoffs, a special night in the vein of Christmas Eve or Easter Sunday for baseball people. I brought Albert a can of party peanuts and a Coke for the occasion. I told him I snuck them in but in truth I okayed it with his doc first. Everything is more fun when it feels like you're getting away with something but I didn't want to kill the poor guy. He thanked me and we sat down to watch the game on the crappy little 19 inch black and white hospital TV that was mounted to the wall. I had a couple of hours before my shift started so I hoped to get three innings in with him before I had to go. It turned out that we would only get one and a third.

The Mets were playing the Cubs and the game was over in the first for all intents and purposes. The Mets put up 8 runs without recording an out in the first before the Cubs got the pen up. It was a total snoozer but Albert and I are true believers so we watched anyway. But even an avid fan can't help losing a little focus watching a totally lopsided game like that one. So we started talking. Since he rooted for the Dodgers and I root for the team named after me and neither of them even sniffed .500 that season we mostly talked about next year. After awhile the conversation ebbed as they often do among friends and then out of the blue he said, "Did I ever tell you I almost played for the Yankees?"

I looked at him with a smirk and said, "Get the hell out of here."

"Scouts honor," he said.

"That is amazing!"

He chuckled and said, "It sure was."

Then he went on to tell me the most incredible story I have ever heard from one of my patients.

In the early 1950's Arkham Falls, like most of America, was a very different place. I won't try to sell you any bullshit notion about the "good old days" because one thing I've learned is that there never was any such thing. But there were different old days. There has always been violence, deceit, broken homes and stupidity of all kinds. But this used to be a nation of producers instead of consumers. We used to make things and we were good at it. It also used to be a nation of communities instead of a nation of households. People got together in person to share common interests. There were clubs and gatherings at various local halls and parks. Modern people think that the place to share common interests is in a chat-room on a website. The idea of actually chatting in an actual room with actual other people instead of some avatar on a computer screen is the furthest thing from our minds. But it wasn't always this way.

One of the most common interests in Arkham Falls in those days was high school baseball. The city was too small for a minor league club back then, though a few have come and gone in the years since. So the men and women who liked the sport would often get their fix at one of the local schools. The best team in the city and in the area was the one from St. Mary's High School.

There were a lot of highly talented players on the Saints. One of them was the 18 year old Albert Quinn. He pitched for the Saints varsity team in 1949 and 1950. In those two full seasons he never recorded a regular season loss going 22-0 with 5 no decisions and 15 complete game shutouts, including 4 no hitters. To say he dominated the high school level would be a fair statement.

On a sunny Saturday morning the week before graduation a shiny green Hudson pulled up in front of Albert's house. The sun glinted off the hood that seemed to be longer than the rest of the car. Albert was sitting on the porch reading a comic and thinking about the algebra final he knew he was going to fail that coming Monday. He looked up from the Sgt Rock adventure at the man who stepped out of the car. The man was wearing a suit and thick eyeglasses. He was staring intently at a piece of paper on a clipboard. The man looked up at Albert and smiled hopefully. Then he opened the gate and came up the walk toward the porch. Albert remained in his seat. He wasn't a rude kid, quite the contrary, but he was sure the man was a salesman and he wasn't in any mood for that sort of interruption.

The man shuffled up the walk and climbed the porch steps. He looked at Albert and said, "Good afternoon son is this 48 Sycamore?"

Albert nodded indicating that it was.

The man looked relieved and asked if he was Mr. Quinn.

Albert said, "Yep, I'm one of them. But I think it's the other one you want. Hang on I'll get him."

Before the man could correct him Albert got up and disappeared through the screen door. The man could hear him heading into the house calling to his father. He leaned on the porch railing and fanned himself with a battered fedora. It was shaping up to be a scorcher of a day though it wasn't even noon yet. He was happy he'd found the kid with relative ease, now he could deliver the happy news and get back to his air conditioned hotel room downtown before he died of heat stroke.

After a few minutes the kid came back with his dad and the man straightened up.

"I'm Jacob Quinn, my son says you're looking for me," Albert's father said as he extended his hand to greet the man.

The man stretched out a pudgy hand and shook. "Well, Mr. Quinn I'm glad you're here but it's actually Albert I came to see."

The two Quinn's looked at each other and then at the man. Jacob said, "Maybe you ought to just tell us what you're selling and get on with it friend."

The man chuckled at that which only served to further confuse Albert and his father. Then the man turned serious as he looked directly at Albert and said, knew the guy as well as he knew himself so it was no comfort at all to see a look of utter terror coming from behind the catchers mask. That's when Albert took it to the next level. He didn't wait for a sign. He knew he was going to have to take the bull by the horns and put his team on his back and that is just what he did.

The kid from Canarsie stepped into the box. He looked like he was 7 feet tall and 275 pounds but Albert didn't care. He looked in at Stan who still looked like a deer in headlights. Then he wound up, reached back and fired as hard as he could right down the middle. It was the fastest four seamer he could muster and it blew right past the swing of the Brooklyn kid's bat and into the glove of a surprised Stan Lapham.

Albert stepped in front of the mound and held up his glove awaiting the return throw and yelled, "Come on Saints let's go!"

His team recognized the passion he was showing and they responded. They didn't play flawless ball but they got through the first clean. When they went into the dugout Albert was very vocal and very positive. He picked everybody up with his tough attitude and after the game even though they had lost his team had found a whole new level of respect for him. The following spring he was unanimously voted Captain.

"So the Yanks want me?" Albert was still shocked. He knew he'd been pretty good, maybe even semi-pro good but this he never expected.

"Well, the Yanks want to see you. We'll put it that way," Schwartz said. He pulled an envelope from the clipboard and handed it to Albert. "Go ahead kid, open it up."

Albert tore it open and unfolded the single sheet of letterhead it held. This is what it said:

```
Dear Mr. Albert Quinn,

          It is with great pleasure that I
write to you today. On behalf of the New York
Yankees Professional Baseball Club I am
extending an invitation for you to attend a
voluntary open tryout for our developmental
league team. The tryout will be held on June
28th, 1950 at 9 a.m. at Yankee Stadium. Please
wear athletic shoes and bring your own bat and
glove.

                         Sincerely
                         Richard P. Grossman
                         Head of Scouting
                         New York Yankees
```

Albert read the note five times each time it felt more surreal than the last. Finally he folded the note and handed it to his dad.

"So I just show up ready to play?"

"That's all there is to it."

"Wow," Albert said and then he just sat back in his chair shaking his head.

Schwartz pulled out another envelope. This one was fatter than the first and heavier. He said, "This is a train ticket and directions to the stadium. It also has instructions on where to go when you arrive. There is three hundred dollars cash in there too to cover any incidentals or emergencies that might arise during your trip."

Jacob who had been silent so far now spoke up. "So this is the real thing, huh?"

"Yes sir, it is," Schwartz said.

"The big leagues," Jacob said and then whistled as he looked at the letter again.

"Well, actually it's the minor leagues but with his talent and hard work anything is possible."

Jacob nodded but didn't say anything for awhile. Albert just sat looking out at the sun soaked lawn with a big goofy smile on his face. He was a million miles away and the two adults knew it. In his mind he was being fitted for his World Series ring already.

After a few minutes thought Jacob started asking the questions he knew his son would never think of and that Schwartz fully expected having heard them all a thousand times before.

"Say the Pittsburgh Pirates come here tomorrow offering the same thing or better. How's that work?"

"I'm glad you asked. Albert is not under contract at this point. We have no legal right to him at all. This is simply an offer to try out. If he gets a similar offer from another club or even a contract offer from another club he is free to pursue it."

"Uh huh," Jacob said rubbing his chin.

"We sincerely hope he comes to work out for the home club of course but he's a free man."

"Yeah," Jacob said. He was still rubbing his chin and thinking. "So what if he tries out for multiple teams and gets multiple offers?"

"Again, he's free until he signs a contract. He can

go with the situation that suits him best."

"Dad, why are you beating him up? It's the Yankees!"

"I know I just want to make sure you have all the information is all," Jacob said and he finally allowed a smile to spread across his face too. The reality of it was starting to set in for both of them now. A kid from little old Arkham Falls had attracted the attention of the most famous ball club in the land.

"Alright Mr. Schwartz," Jacob said as he stood up and offered his hand again. "I'll make sure he's there come hell or high water. Thank you for coming."

Schwartz shook his hand. "The pleasure was mine." Then he turned to Albert and shook his hand too. "You take care of that arm son. It just might be your ticket to greatness."

With that the man picked up his things and turned toward the steps. He shuffled away the same way he'd come. He fired up the big green Hudson and drove off down Sycamore Street. Once he was out of sight Albert looked at his father with the same big goofy smile he'd worn since the man had handed him the card. Jacob hugged his son tight. He had never been as proud of anything in his life as he was of his son at that moment. Their joy would last exactly one week.

Albert's mother took the news well, for her. She brought her hand to her mouth as she read the letter in the kitchen. Stark sunlight flooded the room setting the apple printed wall paper, apple printed curtains and porcelain apples in the bowl on the table aglow with heavenly light. When she finished the letter her eyes were filled with tears and all she could manage in the way of speech was to gasp, "Oh Albert, oh honey," over and over again.

She planned dinners to celebrate for the entire week ahead. Monday evening she would invite Coach Young over along with a few of Albert's teammates, Tuesday would be for his grandparents, Wednesday would be for the pastor, and so on. Mrs. Quinn celebrated all special occasions with dinner parties it was just her way. Albert and Jacob smiled to themselves as her stupor over the letter burst and she began frantically rushing around the kitchen planning. She was talking to herself about the scattered logistics that would determine the success or failure of the week's festivities. She started rummaging through cupboards spouting out a list of things she would need from the market intermixing that list with the guest list and addresses of the people on it and all the while the men watched in good humor taking it all in. To even attempt to help her would be futile and they knew it. So they assumed the role of spectators.

The week went as Albert's mom had planned. Everyone who came over was very proud that all of Albert's hard work had paid off and they were happy for his good fortune. As word spread through Arkham Falls that one of its sons was headed for a big league tryout congratulations letters began to stream into the Quinn mailbox as well. Every day that week it was bulging when Albert got home from school. He was glad for all the well wishing but he was beginning to feel embarrassed by the attention. Thursday afternoon he decided that he needed a break.

He arrived home from school just before 4 o'clock, he was feeling relieved. His last class of the day had been math and Mr. Howe had ended the day by handing back the graded tests from Monday. Albert scored a 78 on his exam. It wasn't anything to shout for joy over but he'd passed and that was really all he could ask for. He was just happy he wouldn't fail his senior year and screw up his shot with the Yanks. Although the idea of dropping out and going after his baseball dream no matter what happened with school had crossed his mind. Such desperate measures would only be taken though if the need arose. He would never have done such a thing without a heavy heart and he never would have even mentioned such a notion to his folks. Now thankfully all of that was moot because he had passed.

Albert didn't take the time to look through the handful of letters he simply tossed them on the table and headed to the garage to get the basketball. He thought he'd head down to the playground and see who was around. A little pick up basketball always helped him blow off steam. But when he got there no one was around. So he shot some free throws for awhile anyway just to clear his head then he took a walk around the park. He sat on a bench for awhile and watched some kids playing kickball. He looked down at the bench where someone had carved "Marjorie Newsome smells like peanut butter" in the wood. Arkham Falls' version of Shakespeare, he thought to himself.

After watching a few innings of kickball he got up and walked home. He had to be there for dinner or his mom would brain him for sure.

When he got home he was greeted by a houseful of wonderful dinnertime aromas. Mr. Davidson his father's boss and his wife were the guests of the night. Mr.

Davidson shook his hand and half jokingly asked about tickets to a few Yankee games if Albert indeed signed with the team. Everyone had a laugh and then sat down for dinner. The stack of mail on the counter was the furthest thing from anyone's mind for the entire evening.

The next day was the last day of school. Again Albert came home and his folks weren't there yet. His dad was still at work and his mom was off picking up a few things to put the final touches on the big party they were hosting that evening for the entire neighborhood. Albert again grabbed the mail and tossed it on the counter. He barely noticed that yesterday's stack was still there too. Again he got his ball and headed to the park for awhile.

When he arrived home his folks were waiting for him as they had been the night before but tonight their mood was very different. The back yard was already full of neighbors and friends. Albert said some hellos as he made his way to the house. When he entered the kitchen and saw his parents faces he stopped in his tracks. His mother was in tears and his father had the most somber look on his face that Albert had ever seen.

"What is it?" He asked, immediately he started wondering who in the family might have died. That's how serious they looked.

"Son, you might want to sit down," his dad said.

Jacob went to the table and took a seat and Albert followed his lead. His mom was frozen where she was, her back resting on the lip of the counter by the sink. She was ringing her apron in her hands nervously as she wept.

"Dad, what is it? Is it Gramp?"

Albert's father looked him in the eyes and shook his head. Then without a word he slid a letter across the table to his son. The letter made a sighing noise as it slid across the yellow Formica. Albert picked it up and read it then when he finished he put the letter down on the table and sat there silently for a long time. After awhile he looked up at his parents and though his eyes were filled with tears he managed a forced smile any way.

In a thick voice he said, "Hey, I just traded a Yankees uniform for a slightly different one right?"

He had just been drafted by the U.S. Army. Instead of going to pitch for the New York Yankees Albert Quinn was going to fight in Korea. Outside his entire neighborhood was enjoying his good fortune. In the kitchen the Quinn family's dream was dying.

* * *

I finished cleaning Al Jr.'s chair then I brought it into the living room to dry out. I poked my head into his room to see how he was doing. He was sprawled out sound asleep just as I suspected. I let him rest; he was going to need it. His dad was a pretty well known guy around the area and most people adored him. This funeral was going to be taxing, especially for a guy as sociable as Al Jr. I already knew how the afternoon would go down, Al would be nice for maybe a half an hour but after that each person who parroted "I'm sorry for your loss" would push him closer and closer to the edge until he'd either go off on someone or he'd tell me to get him the fuck out of there, and those are the exact words he'd use too. A nap would help to extend his patience at least enough to get through the family members. I'd just have to hope for the best after that.

I set about getting Al's suit ready which took all of fifteen minutes. I laid it out on the sofa in the sitting room next to his wheel chair then I went to the kitchen and poured myself a finger of Beam.

I took the whiskey back to the sitting room and flopped down on the couch. Al would wake up in the next hour or so. Until then I was going to chill out and get myself mentally prepared for the afternoon. I am much more socially conscious than Al but keeping him in check can be exhausting, I thought it would be best to go into the ring fresh.

I looked out the rain soaked window that Al loved so well. Again my mind went back in time to memories of Al Sr. He told me he spent three years in Korea without a single thing happening then shortly before he was set to come home the shit hit the fan. But I'll get to that part soon enough.

The night he received the draft letter Albert sent a letter of his own to Walther Schwartz, the scout from the Yankees who had brought him the invite. He explained the situation and informed the Yankees via Schwartz that he would unfortunately not be attending the tryout but he hoped that the offer might still stand after he fulfilled his duty to the Army. A funny thing happened after that.

Albert went to basic training and was set to go to infantry school from there as per his orders. But before he could ship out new orders came down for him suspiciously at the last possible moment. He said it was like something you'd see in a movie, like a fictional Deus ex machina or something. But he assured me it wasn't made up. He said he never found any proof that the

Yankees were behind it but he always suspected that they were. But whatever force was behind the change Albert would now be trained to work in the motor pool instead of the front line infantry. Albert spent his time in Korea learning everything there was to know about jeeps, tanks, personnel carriers and every other motorized vehicle the Army owned. It was going to be very valuable knowledge for him to have later on.

His tour went on from there without a hitch. That is until someone behind a desk in some Quonset hut on some army base somewhere decided that a forward unit in the northern part of the country needed a new shipment of jeeps. The jeeps arrived on a ship and were driven to Albert's motor pool. His CO ordered Albert's unit to drive the six jeeps to the base on the front line where they would drop them off. Afterward they would return in a two ton truck which would follow the convoy of jeeps north. Albert was assigned to drive one of the jeeps and his buddy Steve Moore would ride shotgun. Steve's job was to keep the snipers, who lived to pick off GIs in convoy formations, from killing Albert and himself.

The trip to the front was completely uneventful. The jeeps made it safely to their new home. There truly is a God after all·I guess. The return trip was anything but uneventful however.

The men all loaded into the back of the truck. They were rumbling south through the Korean country side shooting the breeze. Most everyone was talking about going home. News had been spreading through the ranks for weeks that an armistice was just a matter of time. This war was all but over and spirits were high.

Albert turned to say something to his buddy Steve when something zipped through the canvas tarp that covered the cargo area of the truck. The bullet poked a hole in the dirty green canvas and slammed into the floor boards at Albert's feet. There was a split second of confusion then everyone realized what was going on. About the same time three more bullets tore through the canvas in rapid succession. One of them hit a kid named Dave Trumbeau, the son of a high school English teacher from Ft Worth, in the right shoulder. The truck rolled to a stop as Dave cried out and grabbed his arm. No one was sure if the truck stopped because the driver had realized they were under sniper fire or if it had stopped because the driver was hit. All they knew was that they were sitting ducks.

Everyone got low and waited to see what would happen next and for a few minutes that was nothing at all.

To a man they wondered what was going on in the cab but from the front of the truck came only silence to answer them. Albert waited a moment longer and then he decided to act. He tapped Steve on the arm and pointed to himself and then to the back of the truck. Steve shook his head but Albert just smiled and gave him a thumbs-up and went anyway. He took his rifle and crept toward the back of the truck as two more bullets ripped through the canvas. No one was hit but it sent a fresh wave of dread through the men. Every eye turned to Albert as he poked his head out through the flap at the rear of the truck.

It was early afternoon and the sun was high. The truck had stopped in the middle of a road that ran through a small valley with shallow mountains on either side of it. They couldn't be in a worse position. They were like the last potato chip in the bottom of the bowl. He looked up at the rocky slopes as best he could without giving himself away. He really couldn't see much at all. He knew roughly what direction the shooter was in from the trajectory of the bullets, he would be on the mountain to the left of the truck. But the truck was parked at such an angle that he couldn't see that slope at all. He would have to get out to take a look. But he would have to be very careful because there was no way of knowing whether or not there was another shooter somewhere else.

Carefully he opened the flap and climbed out onto the gravel road. He stayed as close to the truck as he could as he moved along what he presumed to be the sheltered side. No shots came so for the moment he felt safe to his rear. It seemed as though the sniper was alone after all. He made his way to the cab and climbed on the running board to peek inside. The driver and the soldier riding shotgun were both hit. The passenger was alive but in no condition to do anything other than bleed and pray. The driver wasn't so lucky.

Albert peered around the cab at the hillside. All he saw were rock outcroppings and a few copses of trees. He would have to draw the snipers fire if he was going to get a shot at him. He climbed down and went to the front fender of the truck. He took a deep breath to steel himself then he very quickly darted out in the open and then back behind the truck. As he had anticipated two quick shots peppered the ground in front of the truck. Albert's heart was pounding but he couldn't help a smirk.

He carefully poked his head up to look across the hood at the hillside. A bullet glanced off the hood just missing his right ear. He played this deadly peek-a-boo game three more times until he had a pretty good idea where the sniper was. Once he was fairly sure about the enemy's location he hit the deck and crawled under the truck.

He tucked in behind the left front tire and peered through the holes in the wheel. He had a decent view of the hillside. In the back of the truck he heard some movement and a yelp from Dave Trumbeau. Albert assumed they were probably trying to give the poor guy first aid for his wound. Good, he thought, they could focus on Dave and he would focus on eliminating the threat from the sniper.

He looked in the general area where he thought the shots were coming from. There was a small pile of rock there. He fixed his eyes on the escarpment and watched for a long time. Finally he saw a very slight movement then the glint of the snipers view finder. Albert sighted in on what was his best guess as to where the man was. He pulled off two quick shots. The man fired back and when he did Albert saw the movement of the recoil. He emptied his clip into the place where the movement came from.

As he reloaded silence filled the little valley. The sulfur smell of gun smoke hung in the air and his ears were ringing from the sharp reports. But no return fire came. It was likely that the sniper was waiting for him to assume he was safe and come out. But whether it was a ploy or not Albert was going to have to test it eventually. He was never one for pussyfooting around a situation even one like this.

He crawled out from under the truck and took cover by the front fender. He leveled the rifle at the sniper's hiding place and stepped out. No shots came.

He made his way to the back of the truck and looked in. The other men were indeed attending to Trumbeau.

"I think I got him," Albert said. "But I have to go up there to make sure."

Steve Moore said, "I'm going with you."

"Like hell you are," Albert said.

"Like hell I'm not," Steve said as he got up and jumped out of the truck.

Albert conceded to let Steve come with him. The two men climbed the gentle slope up to the sniper's nest. When they approached the rock formation it was clear right away that the threat was no more. There was blood everywhere and when they stepped up on the stones and looked down into the little pocket the man had been hiding in they saw what was left of him lying in a pool of blood and staring blankly into the sky. Steve looked at Albert and said, "You saved our lives."

Albert didn't say anything. He just turned and walked back down the hill to the truck. He had Steve help him get the injured soldier out of the cab and into the back where the other men could see to him and Trumbeau. Then they performed the grizzly task of removing the driver. They put him in the back with his wounded brothers. Then as they had done on the trip up there Albert drove and Steve rode shotgun. They returned to base without further incident.

A week later the Battalion Commander awarded Purple Heart Medals to the wounded men and also one to the fallen driver. In the same ceremony he awarded the Bronze Star to Alfred Quinn. Not long after they were all on their way home as the troop withdrawal began. The Korean War was over.

Albert was a hero but he didn't feel like one and when he got home the feeling only got worse. The reception wasn't like the ones he'd seen as a kid when WW2 ended. This time the war weary nation just kind of shrugged and said welcome back then moved on with their lives.

Albert contacted Walther Schwartz about a second shot at the tryout. Schwartz's response was immediate but it wasn't good news. The team had moved on in his absence and Schwartz was sorry to say that they had no need at that time but he also hoped that Albert would stay in touch. Albert was dejected but he didn't give up. With the help of his high school coach he contacted the manager of the Manchester Peaks, a bus league club from Vermont. It wasn't the Yankees, not by a sight, but it was pro ball.

The team toured northern New York and New England and played from June until September. Albert got a tryout and although he was rusty he still made the team with no trouble. For the next three years he lived on a bus and in sketchy motels all over the region. He pitched well though he never returned to the dominant form he'd had before. The hitters were better, the conditions were worse but in truth he just didn't have the same approach he'd had before. He felt older, the war had changed him. It'd also made him grow up and all of the traveling and playing games felt different to him now. It felt like kid's stuff. He began thinking more and more that maybe he should go back to Arkham Falls and start living a more responsible life. Sure he was a good enough pitcher to keep his gig in the minors but it was becoming clear that the minors are where he would stay. Did he really want to be a 40 year old broken down pitcher with no other job skills one day? The more he started asking himself that question the more the answer became clear.

So he finished his third season with the Peaks then he got his last paycheck. He took it home to Arkham Falls and used it and a small loan from his dad to start Quinn's Quality Used Cars. He started out with a little single room cinder block sales office and five cars that he got for a song at auction. Five years later he had three locations and he was grossing six figures. Ten years later he was the largest Chevy dealer in Upstate New York and a rich man. It wasn't the Yankees but it wasn't too bad either. Albert Sr. knew how to make lemonade like nobody else I have ever known.

It was time to get Al Jr. up and get him dressed. I stubbed out my cigarette and grabbed the suit from the back of the couch. I made my way down the hall to Al's room. He was awake already when I went in. He was looking through some old pictures he had stashed in a shoe box. He didn't look up when I came in he just kept shuffling through the snapshots slowly and pensively.

I brought the suit over and laid it on the bed next to him. I put my hand on his shoulder and said, "Al if you want to start on the suit I'll go get your chair."

He nodded and I turned to go. As I reached the doorway he said, "Did I ever tell you about the car, Ray?"

I turned back. "What car is that, Al?"

"The one that made me like this," he said and nodded at his legs.

I had a vague understanding of what had happened to Al Jr. from what I'd picked up here and there over the years but I didn't really know the whole story. I knew that he was paralyzed from the waist down and that he wasn't born that way. He'd had some kind of accident when he was a teenager and it involved a car. But that was the extent of the facts I had on the subject.

I went back over to the bed and Al handed me a picture. It was an old Polaroid that was faded with time. It showed Al Jr. and Sr. together. They were leaning on the front fender of an old Corvette. It was the second generation style from the mid 60's and it was in terrible condition. But Al and his dad were smiling ear to ear in spite of the condition of the car.

"I'd like to say nice 'Vette but I'd be lying," I said.

Al smiled a little. "No it was a piece of shit from the get go. But I thought it was the greatest thing on wheels. I was kind of a dumb kid; I fucked around a lot in school you know? I liked getting laughs more than I liked getting grades. I figured life was about how much fun you could get out of it and all that other bullshit just got in the way. But the old man was cut from a different roll of tape. He was a go-getter, Army hero and business man and shit. Anyway he tried everything to get me to shape up. He was worried I'd end up dropping out and run off to follow the Grateful Dead around or something."

Al laughed to himself and then kind of faded away into the pictures for a few minutes. He said nothing for a long time as he continued to flip through them.

After awhile he said, "That car was how he finally got through to me. I was in my senior year and it was coming up on Christmas break. I got my grades from school and they weren't good. I was passing Gym and Auto Shop and that was all. Well he saw the grades and he blew his top. After he calmed down he said to me 'Jr., I know just what to do with you. You are the type of guy who isn't afraid of nothing', he said. 'That's a good thing but it also is a bad thing. You can't punish a guy that isn't afraid of anything. So I'll make you a deal. You pass in school and I'll help you get a Corvette.' Well I just about hit the God-damned floor. Here I am thinking he's gonna belt me up side the head and he tells me this instead. Shit!"

"I bet you thought you'd won the lottery," I said.

"Something like that, yeah," Al said.

"So you pulled it off I assume."

"Oh sure, I cheated like a motherfucker to do it but I pulled it off."

We both laughed at that. Then Al went on, "Those passing grades probably cost me more than the price of the car. I was into everyone I knew for math test answers and social studies homework, you name it. But all that didn't matter, it was a challenge and while I obviously don't face challenges with the same moral code as the Old Man I do share his fire for facing them!"

"So you got the car."

"I got the car. In June the final grades came out and I was a straight C student. The Old Man smiled and clapped me on the back. Then we loaded in his truck and he took me to the repair shop at his dealership here in town. We got out of the truck and he led me around behind the shop and one of his guys, Frank Taylor was standing there next to a car under a tarp. I looked at dad and then at Frank and smiled. Frank nodded and stepped away from the car. I ran over and yanked off the tarp and that hunk of shit 'Vette was sitting there looking like chrome plated heaven to my 18 year old eyes. Dad said it was all mine. We stood by the fender and Frank snapped that picture," he said nodding at the old Polaroid I held in my hand.

"That's good stuff," I said.

"Yeah but it turned to shit fast. The car needed work as you can see. But that was no big deal; I mean the Old Man owned a Chevy dealership. I had all of the best 'Vette mechanics in the city at my disposal. So every chance I got I'd go down to the shop to work on the car and pick the brains of the guys about whatever the hell I'd found wrong with it, which I can tell you was quite a bit.

"One Saturday morning early that summer I was at the garage working on the car. There was no one else around since the place was closed up. That was always my favorite time to work in the garage. It was peaceful being in there alone with just me and my work you know? I remember reading Zen and the Art of Motorcycle Maintenance when I was younger and the guy said something about how he loved working in a quiet shop too. Some people like to have music blaring or a lot of conversation while they do this kind of work. But he didn't, he liked the peace and quiet and the tactile pleasure of the work itself. That's how I always was too. Anyway I was almost done with the car. I'd spent two months and God knows how much money getting it fixed up but it was almost done.

"I was doing back brakes on it that day, I'll never forget it. Fucking Bendix brakes are a bitch because while they should be uniform they never are, every make has different springs or something. Anyway I had the wrong spring compressor so I had to go to the toolbox to grab a different one. The car was on the lift so I just walked under it over to the box like I had done a million times before only this time God decided to play a practical joke on me. There was no good reason that I know of for that car to fall. It was on the lift in exactly the same position as always, but it fell anyway. I once heard a joke, 'there's a reason for everything and it's usually physics'. Hysterical, right?

"Because I was alone I laid there under that God forsaken piece of shit for three hours. Not that it mattered anyway. The spinal injury was instantaneous, I was paralyzed the second the car hit me. But the Old Man just happened to stop by around noon to see what I was up to and he found me like that."

He stopped there for a moment. Tears were streaming down his face. I said nothing. I knew he needed to tell this story and he needed to do it at his own pace. Finally after a few minutes he went on.

"He blamed himself. That's the worst part of it all, Ray. He thought it was his fault. He blamed his lift, his shop, the fact that he bought me the car, the fact that he wasn't there helping me, all he saw was his own fault in the thing." He pounded his fist in his lap. "God damn it he was my HERO!"

I knew what he was going through. Regret is a weight you can't just put down and walk away from.

"It was an honest accident but he just beat himself up over it. He took care of me the rest of my life. He got me the best care money could buy. He bought me this frigging house and decked it out and I hate every single stick in the fucking thing, Ray. I hate it! Because it all reminds me of how that one second of time ruined my father's life. He was the best man I ever knew and he spent the last twenty years living with guilt over something that wasn't his fault. It was nobody's fault. What the fuck is…"

Here he broke down entirely. I held him in my arms. He sobbed into my chest for a long time. No more words were spoken. What could be said? There was no explanation, no comfort to be had. The random nature of life had haunted the Quinn's since the day the draft letter had arrived in 1950, probably since before then even, just as it haunts us all. There was no way to make any of it better or to make any of it logical. It was like Kennedy's magic bullet, it defied reason but it is what it is.

I comforted my friend in silence and after awhile I proceeded to get him dressed for the funeral. He looked sharp in his suit despite the ratty pony tail and tear stained eyes. It'd be awhile before Al was himself again but I'd be there with him through it all.

The church was packed with rain soaked funeral goers when we arrived. I walked beside Al as he drove his chair up the center aisle of the church. Whispers of recognition, rumor, grief, or whatever followed us down the aisle. The preacher said some words out of his book and tears were shed by the people who thought they got it but didn't. Then when the ceremony was done the preacher invited Al to say a few words. He was the last surviving Quinn and it seemed appropriate that he should eulogize his dad. Al handed me a piece of yellow notebook paper and nodded toward the altar. I leaned toward him and whispered, "You gotta be fucking kidding me. You want me to do this?"

Al just looked at me and nodded. He's lucky I love him.

I went to the altar and unfolded the piece of paper. The statement was brief and in Albert Sr.'s careful hand writing. I was taken aback by that. I expected this to be something Al had written but it wasn't. It was a note from Albert Sr. himself. I read it silently first and then bowed my head fighting back tears. Once I'd gathered myself I spoke into the microphone for the benefit of the congregation.

"Thank you all for coming. I'm Ray Walker a long time friend of the Quinn family. Albert Junior has asked me to come up here to offer some words for his father and I can't think of words more appropriate than those written by Albert Quinn Sr. himself."

I smoothed the paper against the lectern and read.

"I have spent my life around cars. They have brought me fortune and they have brought me the darkest pain I've ever known. If you are hearing these words then the day of my passing has come. After all I've been through I wondered a few times if it ever would. I have narrowly avoided this day several times as some of you know. The long road of life has many exit ramps and sometimes they aren't clearly marked. It would be all too easy to take the wrong one. The road is filled with peril, dangers just waiting to throw us into the ditch or a spinning fiery crash. But the most amazing thing on the road of life is all of the other cars. Everybody here has one. Each person maintains theirs in his own way. Each person drives theirs in his own way. But we all share this road. We are all driving to the same destination and it is only the cars that make us unique."

When I finished I folded the paper up and tucked it into my jacket pocket. I looked out at all the faces for a moment then I said, "Albert Sr. hired me three years ago to be a home aide for his son Albert Jr. I have grown to know this family very well in that time. I know a lot of their story, which is an amazing one to say the least. Albert Quinn was the bravest most honorable man I've ever met. Life threw more curveballs at him than it had a right to and he met every challenge head on. He turned every bad break into a new opportunity. He never backed down from anything ever. Many times I have thought to myself that I wished I was half the man he was. He was and still is an inspiration to me and I am honored that he chose me to look after his son. I could never fill his shoes in any capacity but gaining his trust isn't something I take lightly and I will honor his memory by remembering that. I hope if you take anything away from this service that it is the knowledge of how positive Albert Quinn was. Any one of the tragedies he faced would have broken most of us but he remained optimistic through all of it. He truly believed that how you react to life is more important than anything else. Character is what makes a man and his was second to none. Thank you for coming."

With that I went back to the front pew and sat down next to Al.

He leaned toward me and said, "That was okay. Can we get the fuck out of here now?"

I smiled and said we could.

Al has done well since the funeral. His heart is broken but it is healing a little every day. We have generally returned to normal. We watch baseball and talk about all the stuff we've always talked about. At least once a day our conversation turns to Al's old man and more often than not those conversations end with us smiling at a memory.

Al is glad I'm writing his father's story down. He feels, as I do, that it is a story that should be told. People need to know about the good guys. And among the good guys Albert Quinn Sr. was one of the best.

Jason R. LaPoint
Glens Falls and Athol, NY
Sometime in 2003-December 7, 2013

Little Fish
Based on actual events

Jamil woke up on the soft dirt floor of the little house he and his family shared. He awoke on the floor because the floor is what he had. Mattresses are an unknown commodity in his little desert village. Many common household items are unknown commodities there. The village is in the northeastern corner of Yemen. It is an area that has largely been forgotten by the outside world. Forgotten that is since the British pulled up stakes years ago and left their "colony" to become the independent nation it had always been before they invaded it in the first place. In the eyes of history T. E. Lawrence became a legend and this little corner of the great Arabian Peninsula became no more than a backdrop for his fame and its people little more than movie extras. But that is always the way. The big fish comes into a pool, eats up all the food and then leaves behind the little fish that are lucky enough to survive. The little fish then go on the same as they always had before only they do so with less.

Jamil knew little of fish though and even less of the British. He wouldn't much care to learn about them either. What he knew was that he had to get water from the town well before it was gone. If he missed out another time his father would whip him raw. So the sight of the mid morning sun streaming into the house caused his stomach to sink. It was at least two hours after sun rise. The well would be crowded with people already.

He jumped up, threw on his shirt and sprinted from the house. He sped through town kicking up plumes of dust as he went.

When he arrived at the well his fear proved to be true. There was an impenetrable wall of people between him and the well. The water would be gone before half of them could fill their buckets, broken jars or whatever they had brought to fill. It had happened again. His father was not going to be pleased. This would make three times in the last two weeks that he had overslept and missed out on water.

He would have to sneak closer to the front of the line. He might be beaten by one of the men in the front for budging ahead but he would be beaten by his father anyway if he didn't bring home water. On one hand was the risk of a beating on the other hand was the promise of one. Jamil chose to gamble.

Using his size to his advantage he slunk among the legs of the adults going mostly unnoticed. There seemed to be some sort of commotion which had captured their attention and he reached the front completely free from a sudden smack of knuckles much to his surprise. Even when he brazenly stepped in front of the next man in line and held out his pail no one seemed to notice. The man was so busy talking excitedly to the man behind him in line that Jamil got his water and scurried away without a second look from anyone.

He briefly wondered what the excitement was about but honestly he was far more interested in his own good fortune.

He rushed back through the village to his own house. He burst into the dwelling holding the pale of silty water out before him like a prize. He was beaming with pride over his success. But when he entered things were as they had been at the well. His father and older brothers were gathered around the table talking excitedly and they barely noticed him when he entered. His mother moved among them preparing the mid day meal silently. The look of excited joy the men wore was not shared by her. She looked far more grave than excited.

Jamil quietly took the pail of water to the table and set it among the lahoh and saltah. Then he took his seat and tried to make sense of what his father was saying the best that he could. He was speaking very quickly and many of the words were beyond the boy's comprehension. But the gist was that a very important event was coming. Someone important would be visiting the village; an Emir, a holy man and leader of great importance. His father was talking about how great the opportunities for Jamil's older brothers would be if they could meet the Emir and what it could mean for the family if they did. He was talking about how much of an honor it was that the Emir had chosen their village to visit. He was talking about the ways in which the village would have to prepare for the visit.

He talked on and on all through the meal and when it was over Jamil was every bit as excited as his father, though he hardly understood why. Through it all his mother wore the same stony look of concern. She only broke it to smile and nod agreement to his father when it seemed like that was what he was expecting her to do.

In the ensuing weeks the village was abuzz. Prayers were said with more conviction. Chores were completed with more pride and the people shared an overall feeling of being more alive than usual. Jamil's village was generally a happy place. Most people, or at least the people he knew, who were mainly other children, were happy most of the time. They didn't realize that they lived in abject poverty because what they saw was all they knew. The richest city any of them had ever seen was Aden, which other than its size differed in no way from their little village. The towering metropolises to the east were mere rumors to them. They had heard of Qatar and Dubai. But these may as well have been the places of fairy tales. No one from the little village would ever know any better if they were. But at that time, in the time leading up to the Emir's visit, the village felt like one of those shining places. It felt important and sacred. Its people felt empowered. Men talked of struggle, and brotherhood. Jamil didn't know what they were struggling against but the brotherhood part he thought he understood. He knew some of what they meant as they spoke of it. He knew the feeling of togetherness and oneness brought on by the love of peers and family. These were good things to Jamil.

But all of the bliss was somehow superficial; there was a certain kind of darkness behind the buzz; a quiet discord lurked among all of the big talk of the men. The darkness seemed to come from the women, especially the mothers. There was no joyful talk among them. There was no excited energy. They simply went about their business as usual. They all did their best to act like they were excited too when the men prompted them. But the truth showed through in spite of their act. They seemed to be hiding in plain sight all of the time. Each one of them with that dark look of foreboding in their eyes that Jamil had seen in his mother's the first day they'd heard of the Emir's visit. The women seemed to know something that the men either didn't know or that they were hiding. But it was clear even to a child that there was more to this visit than met the eye. The Emir may be coming as a spiritual leader but a different sort of energy would also be following him to the village.

When the day of the Emir's visit finally arrived Jamil, like the rest of the family was up before dawn. His anticipation made it nearly impossible to sleep at all but he had managed a few hours. He arose from his spot by the window and put on his shirt and sandals. As the family sat eating breakfast his father was oddly silent. He had been talking almost non stop for weeks but that morning he was reverent. His mother still said nothing and still looked grim when no one was paying attention to her. His brothers simply ate their meal.

After breakfast they went out to the village square and joined the excited throng of their neighbors. They waited; each person present could feel the electric atmosphere of anticipation. Those who dreaded the visit as well as those who desired it were equally on edge. Then finally after what felt like an eternity they heard the rumble of approaching engines. In the desert silence is broken from far away. So it was still a few minutes before the trucks finally rolled into the square. But when they did the crowd erupted into cheers and chants.

There were three trucks. The bed of each held four or five men with machine guns. There were also armed men in the cabs along with the drivers. And in the middle of the seat of the second truck was a man with a long salt and pepper beard who could only be the Emir. As excited as Jamil was to finally lay eyes on the Emir he couldn't help but wonder about the armed men. Surely he had seen his share of men carrying machine guns in his life. But he had never seen this many of them in one place. And in the past two weeks he had mentally envisioned the arrival of the Emir many times but it had always been angels or robed wise men who had escorted him into the village, never a small army of soldiers. For the first time Jamil seemed to understand a sliver of his mother's apprehension. In that moment he saw a glimpse of truth. It was a truth he couldn't really understand on any academic level and it wasn't something he could articulate, but the sense of it was there for him just the same. This man came in the name of God. But he certainly wasn't God Himself.

    The trucks rolled to a stop not far from the well. The cloud of dust that had followed them into the village dissipated into the blue sky above the chalk white buildings. The crowd became silent as they waited for the Emir to show himself. The men jumped from the trucks and formed a perimeter around them. Then the drivers and guards climbed from the truck cabs followed by the

Emir himself.

The people of the crowd began prostrating themselves and chanting the Al-Fatiha in unison.

"In the name of Allah, the Most Gracious, the Most Merciful. Praise belongs to Allah, the Lord of the universe. He is the Most Gracious, the Most Merciful. He is the Master of the Day of Judgment. It is You we worship; it is You we ask for help. Guide us in the straight path. The path of those You have blessed, as opposed to those who incur wrath and have gone astray."

The Emir scanned the crowd for a moment. He let them recite the sacred words four times through and then he raised his hands to silence them. All of them obeyed and again the people of the village fell silent. Then he began to speak.

"Children of Allah, it is with great news that I come to you today. The time of the Judgment is upon us!"

At that a nervous murmur ran through the crowd, but as if he had expected as much the Emir simply smiled and went on.

"But fear not for you are holy and faithful. You have been true to Him who shall oversee the Judgment.

You have paid the prescribed alms and kept up with your prayers. And now you will be the foot soldiers in the army of the righteous."

He paused and made a lap around the trucks. He looked in the eyes of the people as he passed them. He looked like a man from out of time. He looked like what Jamil had always imagined Muhammad himself would look like; sandaled feet dirty from all of the time spent walking the desert preaching the Good Words, white robes billowing around him in the breeze, a long grey streaked black beard and soft benevolent eyes. He was exactly as he should be.

"My friends a threat against us has arisen in the far west. There is a kingdom of non believers, sinners with no desire to repent. In this kingdom the people live in towers that reach to the heavens like the Tower of Babel once did. Here they pray to electronic gods. They fornicate in the streets. They are a mockery to their own spoken belief in the holy gospels. All of which surely is bad enough. But their worst crime is against holy Islam. They persecute our brothers who live in their kingdom. They invade us in our home lands, why even at this moment there is an invading army in the west in this very country. But worst of all they burn the holy Qur'an in the streets."

He paused there for a moment to let his words sink in. Jamil didn't own a Qur'an. There were only four in the entire village. It wasn't for lack of piety; most people here simply couldn't afford books- even the most holy book. But those who had it shared it freely. One was in the mosque at the edge of the village that their Imam read from at Friday prayer. The other three were owned by some of the wealthier families. These like the one at the mosque had been passed down through generations and were old enough that no one knew just how old. So the thought of burning it hurt Jamil on two levels. At the forefront of course was the sacrilege of burning the word of God. There was no bigger sin, no bigger affront to Allah than to willingly destroy his most sacred gift to mankind. Secondly Jamil simply couldn't fathom wasting the privilege of having a book- any book at all. This kingdom to the west didn't seem like a very good place to Jamil. And what the Emir said about them having an army here simply terrified him.

"But again I say fear not!" The Emir continued, "For while these infidels are at this moment amassing an army against us in our own land, while they are trying to break our spirit and our very faith!" He paused for a moment and shook his head defiantly. "We have an answer. We have this," he said as he thrust his own Qur'an into the air above his head.

The people cheered and some shouted, "Praise, Allah!"

The Emir went on, "And we also have our own army. The dark cloud of the infidels in the west cannot comprehend the awesome strength of our brotherhood. For right now as I speak to you our forces are gathering. Our own cloud is forming and it is a cloud of holiness and righteousness. A new nation is on the horizon and it is the holy Nation of Islam. This nation is rising and will bring with it a new world. It will be a world based on this law," he said as he again thrust the Qur'an skyward. "The arbitrary laws of man will no longer be the force that drives us from Allah; instead the word of Him will drive us back to Allah!"

Again the people of the town erupted into chants of, "Praise, Allah!"

The Emir smiled and the soldiers milled about. As the speech snared the crowd more and more, the soldiers seemed to relax. At first they had been on high alert. Each man was watching the crowd suspiciously and holding his rifle at the ready. Now almost all of the guns were strapped over shoulders and a few of the men were toeing the dust as the Emir spoke.

"And this nation will be your nation! The next great empire will be the new Islamic Empire. No more of these sinful hordes from the west. No more of the all-talk warmongers from the north, from here on it will be the armies of Allah that spread across the earth. Our army will bring order and faith instead of stealing the riches and laying waste to the bounty of the Earth. Pride will be replaced by prayer. War will be replaced by obedience to Allah and peace will be ours at last!"

With that the Emir walked over to one of the drivers and spoke only to him as the crowd erupted into cheers. The driver signaled to the guards and they surrounded the Emir and lead him off. Jamil's father tapped his brothers on the shoulder and nodded in the direction that the Emir had gone. The three of them and most every other man in the square followed.

After a few minutes the women and children slowly dispersed. As they walked home Jamil's mother was silent. She walked ahead of him her eyes to the front, staring a thousand miles away. She knew what the speech had really been. This was no prayer meeting. This was a recruiting call. It wasn't Allah that the Emir had brought to her village. It was war. But Jamil knew none of that. He was filled with a churning sea of emotions.

He was terrified of this army to the west. He was disgusted by the kingdom from which they came. He was enthralled by how the Emir had stirred his faith. He was proud of his new nation and excited for the day when they would rule the world. In short Jamil wanted more than anything to follow his brothers to the Emir and join the quest. He wanted to follow this man to the end of the earth. He wanted to be a part of the reckoning that was to come. But instead he was forced by his age to follow his mother home and wait for his father and brothers to come back and tell him about it.

He waited patiently for them to come home. He was so excited that he didn't notice his mother nervously pacing the house right along with him. Shortly after sundown they finally returned. Dinner was ready when they arrived but the food was barely touched. Everyone was hanging on every word Jamil's father was saying. He said the Emir told them of the long war that had been raging with the west and how it had touched nearly every country in the Muslim world. Jamil knew of some of the places his father mentioned. But it was a vague knowledge, names with no real substance behind them; Egypt, Libya, Iraq, etc. He knew they were neighboring countries but anything beyond the village really meant little to him. But the Emir said these nations had all come under attack from the west. Each one had faced either covert western meddling or outright invasion. The evil kingdom had attempted to crush the Muslim people and bring them under its reign. But a fire was spreading and the west could do nothing to stop it.

In each place where western oppression had been felt the people had risen up to repel it. In all of these places there were strong successful movements being led by the people to install Islamic governments and Shariah Law. In spite of the efforts of the aggressors the people were taking their countries back.

The Emir said that the time had come to do the same here in the Yemen. The time had come to repel these invaders. This was our land. For millennia our people have lived on these sands. We have lived here, prayed here and we have died here. To allow these vagabonds to take it from us would be an affront to all who went before us. Not to save it would be a sin against our ancestors and a sin against Allah. The Emir asked the men of the village to join the movement. All who were willing to fight to save their land were welcome to join him. Not a man present refused. The Emir said he would return in two weeks with all the tools they would need to arm the village for its defense.

When his father was finished talking Jamil's mind raced. His father and brothers were warriors. In all his life he had known them only to be farmers, shepherds or craftsmen now they would be warriors. Such an honor was intoxicating and again Jamil wished he were just a few years older. He envied them mightily. Any army foolish enough to cross the desert against them would be crushed by his enthusiasm alone if only he could fight along side the men. But for all of Jamil's zeal and that of his father, Jamil's mother could no longer hide her fear. As Jamil's mind was filled with images of himself racing across the sand on horseback, saber raised and wind in his hair, his mother began weeping softly.

Her husband stood and rushed to her side. What was this? He was concerned that she was injured or in pain. He could not conceive of the truth behind her tears. He would never understand that where he saw honor and triumph in the future that she saw only death and suffering. The words of the Emir stirred in her no fervor. Instead, they terrified her. But she said none of this. She knew that he would never understand. She knew he would never be deterred. She simply wept as her husband held her and never knew why. It was better that way.

The following two weeks dragged by. The anticipation of the Emir's second visit was more agonizing than the first time. Then, finally the time arrived, but unlike the first visit this one was accompanied by no showy entrance. In fact most of the village wasn't even aware when the Emir arrived. This time he came in the middle of the night and as per the plan he had shared with the village leaders, only a few men met him.

The Emir arrived with one pickup truck which carried him a driver and a guard and a two ton military cargo truck. The second truck had a four man crew. One driver, one guard and two armed men who would help offload the weapons. The rest of the Emir's men were spread out in a perimeter around the town. They were far enough out in the desert among the rocky hills and dunes that no one in the village could have seen them but they were close enough to be there in a few minutes if they were summoned. The Emir looked on as the men unloaded the cargo; thirty AK-47 rifles, 15 RPG launchers and several cases of grenades and ammunition for the rifles. It was a small arsenal but for a village of just under two hundred people it would be enough to get them started. More shipments would come when they were needed, or so the Emir assured them.

Jamil's father was one of the men assigned to meet the Emir. That night when Jamil heard him go out for the rendezvous he quietly got up and snuck out to follow him. This was just too much temptation for a young boy to resist. The intrigue alone was bait enough to get him moving, the added enticement of the Emir's rabble rousing and his own father's excitement pushed him over the edge. He was a few minutes behind his father as the man made his way through the village to the meeting place. Jamil hid in the shadows and stayed just far enough behind to see where his father was going.

There was a large shed on the edge of the village that the Red Cross people had built to store relief supplies, food and medicine. The shed was all that remained now. The Red Cross like, the UNICEF people, Peace Corps and several missionary groups before them, had all come and gone. The few sheds and dried up wells they'd built were all that remained of their efforts to save the poor little desert village. All of the best intentions of these outsiders had been beaten down under the sweltering heat and poverty of the southern Arabian desert. But Jamil and his people, the little fish, carried on the only way they knew how. There was no helicopter waiting to relieve them from this place. There was no other home to return to, no land of TV and city streets. This was the known universe. The sun in the day, the stars at night, a belly that needed to be filled and a thirst that could never be satisfied, that was the life that Jamil knew and no one from outside, no matter how intent on helping his people they might be, could ever endure it for long.

Jamil crouched down in the shadows as he watched his father enter the shed. A few minutes later he heard the rumble of approaching engines. Two trucks stopped in front of the shed and a group of men jumped out. The guard from the Emir's truck nervously scanned the area as he led the Emir into the shed. He never saw Jamil, none of them did. The men unloaded several crates and brought them inside. Once they closed the door to the shed Jamil waited a few more minutes before sneaking up to the building.

He crept around the side away from the trucks hugging close to the cool wall of the building as he went. He ducked beneath an open window and crawled to where a square of light fell on the sand. He crouched under the window and listened to the hushed voices inside. His heart was beating in his chest like a trip-hammer. He was terrified of being caught but his excitement over what was taking place overpowered that fear twenty-fold. His father was a hero in his eyes and he wanted to be any part of it that he could be.

"Brothers, these are the tools of revolution," the Emir said. "Tomorrow I will send five soldiers to this village to train the volunteers. They will show you how to use the weapons and give you some basic information about tactical combat. You will also receive a briefing about the enemy you are arming yourself against. It is a great honor you are bringing upon yourselves and your village. You are all a part of something bigger than you could ever imagine."

Jamil's heart was swollen with pride. To hear his own thoughts come from the Emir's mouth made him all the more proud of his family. Tears welled in his eyes as he listened to the men inside. He was so focused on the men's voices that he barely heard the buzzing coming from somewhere in the night beyond the glow of the light. But after a moment he did hear it.

It was a faint humming sound like a swarm of bees bearing down on him. Jamil peered into the black trying to see what it was. After a moment his eyes adjusted to the darkness but still he couldn't see anything other than sand and the black sky which sat upon it. The men inside talked on. None of them had heard a thing. Jamil wanted to get his father but he knew he would be in a world of trouble if he did. Instead he sat patiently listening to the sound.

He listened silently for a moment willing his pounding heart to quiet down. He allowed his eyes to follow his ears to the source of the sound. He gazed intently in that direction. Then he saw the thing. It was a slight movement, no more than a wink in the darkness. But once he saw it he couldn't unsee it. Something was indeed flying toward him from out in the desert.

It traveled just above the ground, at roughly the height of a small child. It was the low altitude of the thing that made it so hard to see. It blended in with the dun colored sand perfectly. Jamil had no idea what it was but he knew it was a machine and he sensed more than anything that it was hostile. His senses were acutely accurate, for just as he opened his mouth to scream a warning to his father a flash of light came from the thing and a sound like the sound of the sky being torn open whisked away Jamil's scream before it could be heard even by him.

In an instant Jamil's world was consumed by fire and the screams of the men inside the shed. An instant later it was consumed by darkness.

The men working the security perimeter heard the explosion. But by the time they heard it they were already too late. As they rushed into the village from every direction the shed was already a burning pile of rubble. Villagers were milling around in confusion and the few soldiers who had survived the attack were dragging burning bodies and pieces of bodies from the remains of the shed.

Next to the military truck lay a row of corpses. Each one a blackened ruin of the man it had been just moments before. One of them wore a black keffiyeh and white robe and was clearly the body of the Emir. The commander of the security forces saw the holy man as he leapt from his truck. As he was running toward the body a woman ran past him screaming, "Jamil!"

She ran to a place just beyond the circle of burning debris and picked up the body of a boy from the ground. No one had noticed him in all of the confusion but his mother spotted him right away. She fell to her knees next to the boy and took up his broken form from the cold sand. She screamed his name over and over. Tears streamed down her face as she rocked her son. The boy's lifeless body lay limp in her arms.

This is the true face of war. War is not the news reel footage of grand armies rolling triumphantly down the streets of some capitol city. It is not an action movie where the good guy drives off the oppressor and saves the day. War is not a story in a history book. War is death. War is always the same. War is a mother weeping over a dead son. War is the savage removal of hope and of life. Never has a war been waged without breaking a mother's heart. War is savagery. War is the ultimate disrespect of life and God. And now that war can be fought by a robot, by a machine with no cognitive abilities, with no heart, with no soul, it will only get worse.

As the boy lay dead in his mothers arms, his face streaked with soot, his chest crushed by the impact of the explosion, his dreams dashed to heaven and his future stolen, the drone buzzed away to the west across the desert seen by no one.

I know nothing of Al Qaeda. Nothing beyond what the news media, the White House Press people and a few brief internet searches have told me, which as we all know isn't much. But I can easily imagine that this is what they are. They are the snake oil salesmen of the Muslim World. Their base is a poverty stricken and under-informed public. They use the peoples' own faith and a slightly exaggerated version of our short comings (very slightly exaggerated, but that is a story for another day) to fire them up. It isn't hard to anger people who already bubble with frustration. Then they promise them recognition and eternal life and there you have the recipe for Jihad. Maybe I'm wrong about all that. But I know I'm not wrong about my little fish theory. I have studied enough history to know that this is the through-line for most of it. The every day lay people in every nation, of every religion, of every ethnicity are essentially the same. The fact is I want the same thing that the people in that Yemeni village want. I want to be forgiven for my own short comings and I want my kids to be safe and happy. All of the worlds little fish are the same. And so are its big fish. Because throughout time they have used us like pawns in a big sick chess match. Making us fight and work for their machinations. The flags change, the faces of the leaders change, but the game doesn't. Power wants more power, wealth wants more wealth and the haves will always use the have-nots to get to the other haves. But now it's different because now we can use drones to fight for us. The people in power don't want to kill off all of the little fish in combat. Because if they do that who will be around to buy all the shit from Wal-Mart that fuels our obnoxious economy? So instead of sending people to war now they can send the robots, which, is great other than the fact that if you misprogram the robot it is still going to blow the target to hell just the same. If that target that the programmer thought was a missile silo was actually an elementary school the robot doesn't care. Bombs away! Or if an innocent happens to be in the way of a legitimate target they amount to nothing but collateral damage. And if that happens it's really no big deal because we can always just keep that news piece from rolling. INGSOC only tells us what they want to tell us after all.

Jamil's story is meant to humanize this new trend. It is very easy for Americans to see a news piece about a drone strike accidentally wiping out an entire village somewhere and then pass the peas and move right on with our lives. That is because to the average person in the western world none of it is real. "The news is just another show." But the sad fact is this stuff *is* real. All those dead kids on the news every night are real kids, like your kids, like my kids. They played soccer earlier that day. They farted and giggled about it. They got pissed at their sisters over something. They fell asleep last night dreaming of being big. All of this only to end up on the news lying in a pool of blood over a stupid fucking war dreamed up by two assholes in offices ten thousand miles away from one another. I have no delusions. I know this story won't change anything. I know it'll probably never be read by more than twenty people. But hopefully there will be more. Hopefully people will get mad about this like I am. Hopefully humility can win out over this senseless violence. Maybe one day the world will finally be run by the little fish. Then maybe we can have a little peace.

Jason R LaPoint

The week of 9-11-13, Thurman, NY and Saratoga Springs, NY

Leviatos

Part 1

The Guide

I have heard that when you wake up at 3:15 a.m. for no apparent reason, it is because some visitor from another realm was lurking over your bed watching you sleep. When you awake at this early hour your rational mind may try to convince you how preposterous that notion is but your more primitive mind - the one that resides more in the nerves of the chest and abdomen than in the brain - knows otherwise. As you get out of bed and shuffle to the bathroom the rational brain is in control. But on the return trip something strange happens and the primitive ferret brain starts to take over. Then, somewhere between the bathroom and the presumed safety of the bed, your steps become hurried and you become certain you can feel the hot breath of something hungry on the back of your neck. You rush the last few steps to bed and duck back under the covers. After a few minutes your pounding heart slowly returns to a healthier pace and the top brain begins to win back control of the situation. Eventually, you might fall back into a restless sleep until dawn (dawn, which brings the real horrors) mercifully comes to save you from the dangers lurking in the dark.

It was after just such an experience one night in the early spring of 2012 that I was laying sleepless in my bed. I had just tucked myself back under the covers to begin my standard two hours of tossing and turning. Falling back to sleep easily after a trip to the head is a gift I've never been blessed with. My wife can get up, pee and be back in bed snoring in less than ten minutes total. At minimum I spend two hours tossing and turning and if I've had a nice little ferret brain fright, like I had that night, it would be full morning before I might actually doze off.

Instead of sleeping I laid there trying to convince myself that every creek and groan that the house made was not some ravenous creepy crawly waiting for me to nod off and become easy prey. To make matters worse it was a full moon. For me there has never been a more reliable harbinger of insomnia than a full moon. Every time that big milky ball illuminates the night sky it also kicks the less used and less controllable mechanisms of my mind into high gear.

With a sigh I resigned myself to the notion that the only sleep I was going to get that night would be the fifteen minutes right before the alarm went off.

I lay looking out the big window in my bedroom at the palely lit back yard. It was a still life painted in shades of grey and a strange yellowish white. It had been a disquietingly mild winter and as was the case for most of the last few months there was no snow. But snow or no snow it was very cold and everything was covered with a sparkling scrim of frost. As I lay there, gazing drowsily upon the frozen scene, I had actually started to doze back off when my eye detected a slight movement out beyond the tree line. It was a very subtle flick among the shadowy trees but in contrast with the utter stillness of everything else out there it was very conspicuous. I assumed it was probably a deer and thought little of it. Paying it no mind I continued with my futile attempt at sleep.

Miraculously my eyes started to flutter again and I began to doze. But a moment later my drooping eyes saw the movement again only this time it was much more pronounced. My fall into the Land of Nod was broken. I was perturbed that my rare success at second sleep had been ruined. I decided to turn over and try my luck at sleeping with my back to the window. I would prefer to take my chances facing my snoring wife rather than the suddenly action packed back yard. But it wasn't to be.

I was just about to flop over for my fourth attempt at sleep that night when I saw what was unmistakably a lantern bobbing around among the trees. My fingers fumbled along the headboard for my glasses. I put them on and sat on the edge of the bed to have a better look. Obviously the source of the movement was no deer. Someone was out there in the woods. But who in their right mind would be out there on a bone cold night milling around in the sticks? I watched for a few minutes, straining to see in spite of the branches and my own astigmatism. Finally after a few moments I saw the source of the light and what it was quite honestly still astonishes me to this day.

I watched the light bob among the trees until it

came to a spot roughly aligned with the middle of my property line. Then a figure in a long hooded robe stooped under a limb and stepped out onto the lawn. Once he was out in the open I saw that he indeed had an old style oil lantern in his left hand and in his right hand he held a walking staff. The man, I assume it was a man although there really was nothing about him to indicate gender, simply stood there in my back yard as I sat looking at him. I was rapt by the peculiarity of the whole situation. Being awakened by a trespasser in the middle of the night is enough to give anyone pause, but this was no ordinary prowler. Lurking around in the woods at night is weird enough, but the robe and the lantern were just plain bizarre.

I'm not proud of it but in that moment I was frozen to my spot on the edge of the bed and I didn't know what to do. I thought about calling the cops but I couldn't imagine what I would tell them. The only thing I was sure of is that I would be a punch line at the local police department forever after a call like that. And honestly, so far the usurper hadn't really done anything wrong, at least not in my eyes. If he started trying the locks we'd have a different issue, but so far he was just standing there.

I sat motionless in the moonlit bedroom waiting to

see what he would do next. Through all of this my wife lay on her side of the bed sleeping peacefully. I listened enviously to her soft snores and wished I could share in her obliviousness. If I could only sleep on command like she can I wouldn't be witnessing any of this. But instead I was locked in this strange spring night's interlude.

For some time he was simply posed on the edge of the lawn like a weird statue. He stood stoically with that old lantern held out before him and the moment seemed to drag out forever. He seemed to be assessing the situation but honestly that is purely speculation on my part. Then he turned suddenly and stared directly at me. It is possible, that he was only looking at the house, or so I tried in that moment to convince myself; after all I could see no eyes, no face at all because of the hood he wore, but I sensed more than anything that he was gazing through the window pane directly at me. Then as if he knew what I was thinking he erased all doubt that I was in fact his focus. He raised the hand that grasped the walking stick and pointed a long boney finger at me. Then he slowly turned his hand over and wagged the finger in that familiar gesture that I clearly understood but had no desire to acknowledge. He was beckoning me to come to him.

In an eerily slow manner he lowered his hand back to his side and again he simply stood there staring at me, waiting. I was frozen by the peculiarity of it all but to be honest I was frozen by pure white hot fear as well. I sat looking at him indecisively as he stood looking back at me for a long time. Clearly this was a standoff. But he seemed unfazed and completely content to wait me out. Perhaps it was fear of what he would do if I ignored him, perhaps it was some sort of mind trick he was playing on me, I can't honestly tell you what possessed me to don my robe and slippers and heed his call, but for what ever reason that is just what I did.

I crept silently out of the room being careful not to wake my wife. Then I tiptoed through the house and slipped out the front door carefully pulling it shut behind me as quietly as I could.

The cold night air hit me like a slap in the face. I crept along the side of the house my feet crunching on the frozen grass and my breath making clouds of frozen moisture in the moonlit air. Whatever brought me out there that night it certainly wasn't bravery. I was shivering as much from my fear as I was from the cold. I walked as if I was on auto pilot to the back of the house and then I stopped at the corner and peeked out on the back yard.

He was still standing in the same spot. He hadn't moved a muscle as he'd waited for me to come outside, for I was now sure that's just what he was doing, waiting, for me. I shuddered again and pulled back from the corner of the house. I rested my head back on the cold siding and stared up at the starry night sky. I feel so small when I look into a clear night sky. To me nothing else seems to put our place as individuals into perspective quite like looking through that window to the cosmos.

I steeled myself and poked my head back around the corner of the house. It gave me no comfort to see that his breath, if he had any, produced no puffs of vapor like mine did. This time he saw me and again he raised his hand to beckon me. Then he turned and ducked back into the woods and started back up the path from where he had come. He didn't wait for me to follow. I can't help but wonder now what might have happened if I hadn't followed. If I had simply gone back inside, taken a shot of bourbon and gone back to bed, would he have been aggressive enough to come in and get me, or would he have just let me go? I'll never know because as his lantern began to bob away among the trees I inexplicably felt my feet begin to follow after it.

I ducked under the same bough that he had and then I found the path. With the aid of the lantern glow I quickly located him and caught up. I got to within six feet or so of him and couldn't bring myself to go any closer. I kept my distance out of fear of course but I was also repulsed by the smell of him. His stench wasn't one of death or rot exactly it was more like the smell of neglect. This pervasive odor was akin to the smell of old books that have been stored somewhere damp and dark. I was however close enough now to get a good look at him in the glowing light of his lantern. The hood still obscured his face but I could tell that he was about my size which made me feel stronger about my assumption that he was in fact a man. His robe was black and made of a material that I couldn't identify. It was something like thin wool, and it was dirty and moth eaten. There were tiny twigs and leaves caught in the nap, no doubt from his journey through the woods from wherever he had come. The walking staff that he carried in his right hand was as ancient as the lantern that he carried in his left. It was bone white and gnarled like rheumatoid fingers. The lantern looked to be brass, though it was old and tarnished. It had four windowed sides and a large arc of wire that formed the handle by which the specter held it.

The peculiar thing about the lantern was that I could see no flame. It gave off a steady glow like a Coleman lantern but it was far too old to make use of any such technology.

The man's gait suggested extreme age. He was every bit the stereotypical image of a druid or a medieval wizard. He was a robed shadow figure. He was the personification of mystery. He didn't speak or acknowledge my presence in any way but somehow I sensed that he knew I would follow him. He simply plodded silently along the path. His lantern bobbed as he walked and occasionally the staff clacked off of a rock, other than that he was a rumor. He left behind no evidence that he was there at all except unfortunately the smell.

We wound along the path through the woods, my guide in front with me trailing behind and giving a wide berth to his malodorous wake. I have spent a little time in those woods. I have never been an avid outdoorsman but every fall I put up a tree stand out there and from time to time my wife and I venture out for a short hike. It is an old forest and there isn't much in the way of undergrowth once you get in beyond the tree line. The forest consists mainly of hoary old pine trees and some scattered maples and poplars. There are some rocks and the occasional moss covered deadfall to trip you up but for the most part it is a fairly clean forest floor. Walking there is so easy in fact that it never occurred to me to actually follow the path much before that night. I had walked on it for a stretch from time to time but I had never really been compelled to follow it to its terminus. I just assumed it went on to some long forgotten point of interest out in the woods. Before that night I never really gave it a thought. Since that night I've thought about it every single day.

The cold was uncomfortable but it became less so as we walked on and my blood started pumping a little more. My terror also seemed to abate as we went on. It is funny how the mind will begin to adapt and accept even the strangest things after such a short period of time. But I must say it was still unnerving to see no puffs of breath and to hear no footfalls coming from him. I wondered not for the first time whether this might all be in my mind. Perhaps I was really still tucked in my warm bed back at the house and this was all nothing more than a strange dream. As if cued by this thought I stubbed one of my toes on a rock. My slipper offered little protection against such trauma and a sharp pain shot up my leg. My guide simply walked on apparently oblivious to my accident. I cursed the rock and him under my breath then I gathered myself and after a minute or two I caught back up with him.

We had come a long way from the house, perhaps as far as several miles. I can't be sure of the distance but suffice it to say we were deeper into the woods than I had ever ventured before that night. We had passed over several small hills and through several shallow valleys. We passed a reedy swamp and a couple of fern filled clearings. A few times the path petered out to a mere rut just wide enough for our feet but for the most part it was a wide clear lane big enough to allow any ATV easy passage. But I saw no evidence that anything motorized, or anything at all for that matter, had been on the path for a very long time.

Finally after what felt like at least two hours of walking my guide simply stopped on the path ahead of me. My tired over taxed mind was drifting freely by that point and he stopped so abruptly that I nearly ran into him. The only thing that prevented me from colliding with him was that awful smell. It was like a force field that surrounded him, a tangible barrier of reek between the two of us. The odor intensified exponentially by the inch. So unconsciously I knew that he had stopped even before my upper mind knew that I knew it.

For a moment he just stood there motionless in the moonlight as he had when he first came into my yard at the beginning of this weird adventure. Then he raised the hand that held the staff and pointed off into the woods. I looked in the direction he was indicating. I strained my eyes and peered into the darkness but alas I saw nothing but pines and shadows and moonlight. I was about to inquire of my ghoulish friend exactly what he wanted from me when all at once I heard something coming from the direction in which he was pointing. The sound was very faint and I initially mistook it for singing. It was far off through the screen of the forest but once I heard it I couldn't deny it was there. I listened closely, leaning slightly toward the sound and I realized it wasn't singing, not exactly, but it was voices and they were chanting something in a soft monotonous rhythm. I could discern no detail beyond that. My guide was no help. He simply stood there pointing toward the source of the sound.

He offered no indication that he intended to lead me any further. But it was clear from his insistent pointing that he wanted me to follow the sound into the woods.

My first instinct was to think that there was no way

I was going into those woods without him. Then as quickly as the thought crossed my mind I realized how incredibly ridiculous it was. In what fantasy did I think that this foul smelling apparition was any sort of protection from any danger that might await me in these woods? Wasn't it he after all who had led me out here in the first place? I had followed this thing through the freezing cold forest in the middle of the night unquestioningly and now suddenly I was going to become cautious. The idea was absurd. So I gathered my nerve, I uttered one final curse at my guide under my breath, and then I turned toward the sound. I took a deep breath and set out in the direction of the chanting leaving him standing there on the path.

After a few minutes of plodding through the frozen leaves and twigs I turned to look behind me. I no longer saw the glow from his lantern. The moon above was now my only source of light. I was grateful not to have the smell around anymore though I would have gladly endured the stench again just to have the lantern back. But that was not to be. So, I trekked on through the woods alone and never saw my strange hiking companion again.

Part 2

St. Vitus Dance

My feet were freezing. My slippers were completely soaked from the frost and they felt like two ice blocks stuck to the ends of my legs. But I was driven through the discomfort by an odd sort of curiosity. It was an overwhelming desire to find out what this was all about.

I continued through the woods drawing ever closer to the source of the chanting. As I did so I could now hear it in more detail. There were many voices and they were distinctly female. They were intoning a rhythmic dirge that wasn't exactly musical by any standard definition of the word. As I crept closer I was now able to hear the words they were chanting but this revelation only succeeded in confusing me further. As I slipped quietly through the trees toward the women this is what I heard;

"Kalhalthea, Ng' holeatea."

"Alma Bryn Leviatos, Bryn Leviatos!"

They were repeating this seemingly nonsensical verse continuously. There were no variations at all, no inflection changes, no other words, just the steady repetitious drone of this queer lyric.

Apprehensively I forced myself to move closer and it wasn't long before I got my first glimpse of the women. I crested a small hill and when I did I noticed the intermittent flickering of light on the trees around me. It was the kind of light that could only come from a fire. I slowed my pace and walked softly on the pine needles that carpeted the forest floor. Even if I had snapped a twig or made some other random noise I don't think they would have heard me. It was unlikely that the women were paying any attention at all to the vacant woods around them, though I wouldn't stake my life on that assumption. I knew far too little about what I was into to be anything but careful.

I silently weaved between the trees. I had gone maybe twenty or so feet from the top of the hill when I was finally able to see the women between the branches and the scene before me stopped me in my tracks. At first I thought my tired eyes were playing tricks on me. So I crept closer then I crouched down behind a fallen tree trunk to get a better look. From my hiding place I saw the most extraordinary thing I had ever laid eyes on. The scene was bizarre enough to make me temporarily forget all about my encounter with the ghostly hiking guide.

At the bottom of the hill below my hiding spot there was a clearing in the woods. About twenty five women and girls were dancing around in the clearing. I call it dancing merely for lack of a better term. In truth it was more like an intoxicated skipping. They flailed their arms and tossed their heads around whipping their hair as they carried out this vile choreography. They danced in a circle, round and round, all of them with wild eyes and distant expressions. They were in various states of undress. Some wore amulets on long strings around their necks others had them on leather straps around their wrists and ankles. A few had symbols painted on their naked torsos and legs, others were simply bare to the world. And all the while as they progressed around the circle they chanted;

"Kalhalthea, Ng' holeatea."

"Alma Bryn Leviatos, Bryn Leviatos!"

The woman who appeared to be leading the procession looked to be about thirty. She had long bushy hair which she was swinging around in a circle as she stomped and droned. She wore a peasant style shirt and nothing else. Her pale skin gleamed in the light as her lithe body bucked and gyrated around the circle. Immediately behind her was a girl of about twelve. The child was clothed except her feet but like the others she had the same vacant glassy look in her eyes as she too intoned the verse and danced along. Behind the girl was a much older woman possibly in her mid sixties. This woman wore only under garments. She had short cropped silver hair. She skipped along in line with the others in a sort of Indian-style manner as she chanted the eerie incantation. She too had that same trance-like appearance as the others. And that's how it was around the circle; women and girls, some in nonsensical states of partial nudity, chanting in unison and dancing in anything but.

The sight of the women was odd enough in its own right but it was the source of the light that amazed me more than anything. What I had mistakenly assumed was firelight was in fact nothing so ordinary at all. It glowed like fire but it didn't flicker. What I had earlier mistaken for the flickering was only the result of the light being blocked and unblocked as the women danced around it. From my new vantage point I could now see that this was so. The light-source appeared to be some sort of glowing stone roughly the size of a picnic table and orb shaped. Strangely the big stone ball didn't appear to be giving off any heat; certainly I was now close enough to have felt any such energy coming from an object the size of this one. Any stone that size would have to be super-heated to give off so much light; at least it would under any sane rules of physics. But it was clear to me that there was nothing sane at all about the scene before me.

In the short amount of time that I had been watching, the light emanating from the orb had grown in intensity noticeably. The light was now bright enough for me to easily see every bizarre detail of the scene. I could now see that a rudimentary circle of ordinary river stones had been built around the perimeter of the glowing supernatural one. Their purpose appeared to be purely decorative. The circle of rocks matched the circumference of the orb perfectly but there was no other obvious connection between them and it. Around the stone circle was a beaten path of dirt upon which the women danced and beyond that a bed of pine needles gave way to the forest beyond. The clearing looked as old as time. The rock circle and the glowing orb looked older than that.

I watched for some time. Evidently my hiking guide thought this was something I needed to see, though I couldn't imagine why. However up to that point nothing about this night had made any sense. So, I couldn't feign any shock at the fact that whatever my purpose here was it was lost on me. I simply acquiesced to sit here and watch the women carry out their strange dance ritual around this parlor-sized version of a star. It seemed to be as reasonable a course of action as anything else. The way this night had gone so far I had quite honestly given up seeking any normality in any of it anyway.

Aside from the light which continued to intensify incrementally as the women danced, all else was still as it had been when I first ducked behind the log. In spite of the brightness I was able to look directly at the light with no difficulty. It in no way hindered my sense of sight like say, looking at the sun would.

As I gazed at the thing I was now able to see an intricate pattern etched on the surface of it. The symbols were cast in relief against the intense glow. I wondered if it might be some kind of alien language. I had thought of the orb as something extraterrestrial from the start. It wasn't any cognitive process that led me to think of it that way, the thing simply felt alien. It seemed highly unlikely that anything like this could be of the Earth.

Something else about the light seemed to be changing too, though at first I couldn't place what it was. I watched for awhile and then it finally came to me. Not only was it brighter but it was also changing color slightly. It had taken on a yellowish hue similar to that of the moonlight and as it changed the etching became more pronounced. I could now see that it was indeed some sort of cipher though the language was nothing I had ever seen before. It was scrawled on the surface of the orb in lines that ringed it like lines of latitude. For a moment I gazed at it in awe, hypnotized by the mysterious beauty of the thing.

The strange coven danced on as I stared at the brilliant orb. The sound of their chanting enhanced the hypnotic hold that it had on me and I felt an odd sense of joy wash over me. I felt as though all that I knew, my worries, my regrets; my entire life was something that had happened to someone else. I saw everything as though I were looking through the eyes of a bystander and all of it seemed so trivial, so small. The entire plight of mankind seemed almost silly somehow like it was a mere flicker in the whole of time and therefore my own plight was even less significant than that. The reverie I felt was incredible. But it was also brief.

A sound split the night like an axe through a china cabinet. The spell was shattered and I came out of the trance abruptly like a man who has been ripped from a wonderful dream by the waling of a fire alarm.

The new sound hadn't come from the women. In fact it hadn't come from the clearing at all. Rather it came from the woods beyond. When I heard it all thoughts of the joyful trance, the dancing women and the weird hiker evaporated. That sound instilled such a petrifying terror in me that any thought at all became impossible.

Part 3

Leviatos

To the west of the clearing lies a vast tract of "forever wild" forest that terminates at a remote stretch of the north shore of the Great Sacandaga Lake. It is state owned land within the Adirondack Park. This particular stretch of rocks and pine trees is completely devoid of any kind of human development. If there is any piece of land in New York State where a human foot may never have stepped, it would be that stretch of woods between the lake and this weird little clearing. It was from the direction of that ancient forest that the unearthly noise had come.

It was a low wet sucking sound not unlike that of a storm drain letting go of a clot, only it was amplified by a thousand times. The women seemed undaunted by the sound though the pace of their chant and their steps had increased.

As abruptly as the noise began it stopped. It was replaced by what can only be described as a deep yawn echoing through the darkness. This was followed by several sharp cracks and the distinct sound of trees crashing to the ground. The sound of falling timber did not abate as the other noise had. Instead it grew louder and faster as whatever was out there crashing through the woods came closer and closer. It was clear that whatever was making that noise was coming toward the clearing, perhaps drawn by the stone, the women or both. It was also clear that the thing was gigantic. As it drew closer the pace of the women's incantation grew faster.

Then, from somewhere in the woods no more than two hundred yards away, there came a guttural roar. It sounded like an entire herd of cattle screaming in a united throe of agony. The wail echoed through the trees around me and on the heels of this awful roar the woman who led the throng let out a cackling laugh that froze my blood in my veins.

The pace of the dancing sped even more now and the women now accompanied their chant with a rhythmic clapping. The stone around which they carried out this queer display was now emitting a deep amber colored glow. This terrible light illuminated the coven as their dancing and singing built in tempo. Feet pounded the earth, breasts heaved and fell as the women bucked and sang casting shadows all around the clearing. All the while the trees continued to fall out in the darkened woods beyond as the thing out there drew closer with every passing second.

"Kalhalthea, Ng' holeatea!

"Alma Bryn Leviatos! Bryn Leviatos!"

My heart was in my throat. I was so terrified that I don't think I could have squeezed out a scream. Even if I could have there wasn't anyone other than the women remotely close enough to hear me. My legs were useless slabs of meat which anchored me to the ground and to my fate. I now knew exactly what petrified with fear meant, because that is exactly what I was. I may as well have been made of stone. Then just when I thought I couldn't be more terrified I saw the beast. If it is truly possible to die from fear I couldn't have been far from that end.

At first all I saw was a silhouette, the fact that it was a silhouette against the moon made it all the more obvious just how enormous the beast was, as if the crashing trees and thunderous footfalls weren't proof enough.

It stopped for a moment and simply stood there, it seemed to be assessing the scene in the clearing over which it now stood. The women continued the ritual; none of them broke their trance for even a moment. Then the thing let out another of those ungodly roars. It was the soundtrack of hell. That sound was a blasphemy that was not of this earth.

The roar echoed away into the night. Then the thing continued its approach as the women chanted away at what was nearing a hysterical pace. It was now close enough to the glowing light of the orb that I could clearly make out all of the terrible details. What I saw froze my shallow breath in my chest. In the other-worldly light of the mysterious amber stone I saw a being that even my worst nightmare could never have produced.

The gargantuan wretch's face was made of an exoskeleton. It looked like the skull of a forest rodent like a fisher or a marten. Set in the middle of the head were two milky green orbs that I assume were the beast's eyes. At the end of its snout were three gaping black holes. The remainder of the face was mouth and most of that was filled with razor sharp teeth.

The head sat atop a disproportionately small neck which had a large disc-like protrusion on the back like that of a king cobra. The neck terminated at a body that suggested that whatever had created this thing had simply given up after making such a grotesque visage.

The body was nothing more than a formless mass of adipose flesh which was covered with a patchy scruff. I saw no arms or legs but the sound of trees falling continued sporadically and occasionally I caught a glimpse of what looked like enormous snakes lashing about in the woods beneath the thing, so I am convinced that it stood upon a mass of tentacles of some kind. The entire repulsive beast's coloration was a pale yellow color similar to that of summer squash.

It stood at the edge of the clearing and gazed down upon it's minions with those soulless green eyes. At this point the lead woman stopped dancing and looked up at the thing. She closed her eyes and smiled. Then a thing occurred, the image of which still haunts me to this day. The woman spread her arms and legs wide and threw her head back. Then she began thrusting her hips in the direction of the beast along to the rhythm of the chants of her sorority. It was the most bizarre spectacle I hope to ever witness. She thrust her hips harder and faster along with the clapping of the other women. With each thrust her feet skidded forward little by little in the dark dirt of the clearing. Through it all she continued to recite the strange incantation:

"Alma Bryn Leviatos!

Alma Bryn Leviatos!"

She chanted it over and over as the others clapped and skipped around the now gleaming stone orb. This frantic ritual went on gathering more and more energy. Now the beast seemed to be gyrating along with the woman. Its gelatinous girth rippled and waved in unison with her every thrust and scream. As this mock intercourse went on and on the stone continued to grow brighter and brighter until I could barely see the women in the clearing for its brilliance. They were swallowed up in a sea of light. But the lead woman was still visible at the edge of the clearing, pounding her hips at the air beneath the beast.

Then three things happened in rapid succession. First the ground rumbled softly as a brilliant beam of light exploded from the stone and shot strait up into the sky. Second the beast threw back its grotesque head and let out a guttural groan that shook the very world around me. Then third, thankfully I passed out cold, if ever there was proof of the mercy of God that was surely it.

Part 4

End

When I awoke it was early morning; daybreak on the land. My head felt like it weighed twenty pounds and my mouth felt like it was filled with cotton balls. It was worse than the worst hang-over I have ever had. I sat up slowly and fought the urge to vomit as a spike of pain sliced through my corpus collosum. The wave of pain and nausea passed and then I slowly stood up.

The air around me reeked of dead fish. I peered down at the clearing below. Images from what I'd seen flashed in my mind, but the women, the stone and the beast were all gone. However, the circle made of river stones was still there and there were footprints in the dirt all around it. Also there was a strange path of fallen trees trailing off into the woods to the west. I had no doubt that if I were to follow that path the fish smell would grow stronger and it would lead me to the lair of the beast. I had no doubt of this but I also had no desire to prove it either.

I stood there for a long time looking at the scene before me. Already my rational mind was trying to explain it away. I was trying to convince myself that there was a reasonable explanation. I had sleepwalked out here and had a strange dream brought on by too much clean mountain air. The trail of fallen tress was the result of a wind storm that had gone undetected because it was so far out here in the wilderness. It all made perfect sense. But my ferret brain wasn't buying it; partly because of the vivid mental images and partly because of that pervasive fish smell. The upper brain might buy some thin explanation but the lower one was no fool.

After some time I stumbled through the woods and back to the path. I went to the spot where my hiking guide had left me alone the night before. I stopped for a moment and scanned the woods around me for some trace of him but there was none. Of course there wasn't, I thought to myself. He had barely been traceable when he was actually there.

After a few minutes I wrote off my search for any evidence to prove that my adventure was not imagined. I set out on the path and made the arduous trek back to my house in Harlan.

The walk seemed to take a week though it was only a couple of hours at most. Finally I saw my house through the breaks in the branches. I left the path and walked across my back yard. The yard was now bathed in early morning sunlight instead of moon glow. I looked back at my footprints on the frosty grass. I followed them with my eyes to where they passed beneath the low bough and into the woods. In my minds eye I saw the apparition of my guide standing there with his staff and lantern. I shook my head against the image and went inside.

My wife was in the shower when I came in. Before she got out I changed into jogging clothes and tossed my filthy pajamas and robe into the hamper. I did a few jumping jacks to build up a little sheen of sweat. If she asked where I'd been I'd tell her I decided to go for an early morning jog. Misleading my wife is not something I like to make a habit of. But I saw no viable alternative at the time and in truth I still don't. Telling her the truth was out of the question. Hell, I don't really even know what the truth is. What had I seen after all? All this time later and I still don't know the answer to that. But whatever it was it deserves to remain in the night where it belongs. In truth I hope that's where it stays. I see no point in making my wife suffer this nightmare along with me. Whatever the hell I saw it will be my memory alone. I can't bear to make her have to live with this horror too.

Jason R LaPoint
Thurman, NY
07-06-2012

The Lady of the Wall

"Do not remember the sins of my youth, nor my transgressions; According to your mercy remember me, for your goodness sake, O, Lord."
-Psalm 25

The sun was beginning to set in the Great Lakes sky. Four boys sat in the early evening glow upon the stone face of a break wall. They watched in silence as the sun sank slowly into the western end of Lake Ontario. Bobby, Carl, Mike and Randy had seen nearly every sunset of the summer from this same spot. But this one was special. It was one they dreaded but still honored every September of their young lives. It was the last sunset of summer vacation. Tomorrow would bring a new teacher, new school work and a new beginning. But for now, for this moment it was just the four of them, free and young. And even though none of them could articulate it all of them knew there was something sacred in the event.

"What do you guys say about riding down to the old sawmill tomorrow after school and hunting up some worms for this weekend," Bobby asked his friends as he sat on one of the giant boulders kicking his feet over the breaking waves below.

A mumbled chorus of agreement rose from his friends. The prospect of fishing the following weekend was thin consolation for the loss of their summer freedom. Bobby had tried to take their minds off of it but he knew how they felt, he felt it too.

The boys were so wrapped up in their own thoughts that none of them noticed the man who approached them quietly and took his own seat on the wall a few yards away. The man wore a long black over coat. The front of it was open revealing a black suit that appeared old and seldom worn. He was an older man of around seventy, with ruddy skin that looked wind-burned.

His hair was as silver as a teaspoon and shoulder length, blowing back under his fedora in the wind. He looked like most of the old men around here. It is the look that a life on the lakes gives a man. He sat down on the break wall and bowed his head silently for a moment then looked pensively out at the horizon.

"You guys think the Lady will be out tonight?" Randy asked, breaking the silence.

When he said these words the man perked up and slowly inched a bit closer to the group of boys. Still none of them noticed him.

"Yeah maybe, her anniversary is coming up soon. She usually gets pretty busy this time of year," Carl answered.

"I don't know I haven't heard anything about her for awhile. It's almost like she disappeared," Bobby said as he skipped a rock across the waves.

After a few minutes the stranger said, "She didn't disappear."

The unexpected interjection startled the boys. The four of them turned their eyes to the old man in unison.

Then he said, "She just found what she was looking for is all."

The man stood up and moved over nearer to the boys. He moved slowly like old men do. The vast expanse of years between him and them seemed to stretch out between them like a tangible thing. He looked each of them in the eyes as if he were sizing them up. They simply stared back at him. The boys were as intrigued by the statement about the Lady as they were the strange old man himself.

He reached in his pocket and pulled out a cigar and a Zippo. He lit the cigar and placed the lighter back in the pocket of his over coat. Then he sat back down on the wall and turned his gaze once more to the lake.

"Did you boys ever hear the Lady's story?"

They all looked at him like he was crazy. Of course they knew her story, it had been told to every kid in town thousands of times throughout their lives.

"Sure," Bobby said, "She was a sailor's wife who jumped off the wall after her husband died in a shipwreck. Everyone knows the story of the Lady, mister."

"Well, everyone knows that story," he said as he stared off at the ever darkening horizon. "But do you know the real story."

Now the boys were really interested. All thoughts

of the coming school year were far from their minds. The mysterious old man now had their complete attention. After all he just claimed to have new information about their town's most famous ghost story.

The boys gathered around the man and took new seats on the old rock wall facing him.

"Real story?" Randy asked.

The old man just nodded never taking his squinted eyes from the horizon.

"Tell us mister," Bobby said, with wonder.

He looked at their eager faces and it crossed his mind to send them home. After all they did have school in the morning, but he knew they'd never go now. And in truth he knew that he had to pass this tale on. He had to tell the story before it was too late. He was in the afternoon of life and these boys were in its dawn. If he didn't tell someone he would take the tale to his grave and one more piece of truth would die with him. That was something he couldn't allow to happen. So he took a long pull on the cigar then he turned his eyes back to the red horizon. Then he told them the story that he had kept secret since he was just a boy like them.

"Ever since I was a young boy I have heard the

tales of the Lady of the Wall. She was a young woman, who in the throes of grief took her own life by leaping from the break wall that rims Oswego harbor. She became crippled by despair after the death of her husband, a young merchant sailor whose ship had sunk in a violent gale. It is said that her spirit has been seen walking on the wall on warm summer nights. She appears to tourists and young couples who come out to the wall around dusk; conveying a warning about the danger that surrounds this place. Some also claim to have seen her from shore on stormy nights, carrying a candle that burns in defiance of the wind and rain. The candle is believed to be a beacon by which her lost love may find her through the storm of the beyond. The story of her suicide is the accepted truth of her demise; I however know that it is not the real story. I know the truth boys and I will share it with you..."

* * *

John looked to the west and took some relief at the site of the pink fire of the setting sun on the horizon. He had always heard, and believed in the sailors' adage, "red sky at night, sailors delight." So a smile crossed his face as he left the dock. He and his crewmates had just been given notice that their ship would depart for Detroit at five the next morning with a shipment of oak timber being relayed from Maine. Good weather would be a good start to the voyage. Tackling one great lake in bad weather would be bad, but trying to survive two of them would be worse.

He walked at an easy pace through the quiet streets of Oswego to a small pub four blocks from the dock where his steamship was now being loaded. Whiskey first and then sleep, he thought to himself as he entered the pub and pulled up a stool at the bar.

The bartender nodded, to let John know he'd seen him come in then he finished pouring a pint for another sailor at the end of the bar. He served the ale with a smile and nodded in gratitude at the sailors tip. Wiping his hands on a rag that hung from his belt he turned and walked toward the end of the bar where John sat.

"Evening Peters, what can I get you this evening?"

"A whiskey will be fine Ken, thanks."

"Looks like tomorrow ought to be a good one," he said as he cocked his head towards the window at the sunset. "Should be a nice day to cast off."

"Should be," John said, taking a swig of whiskey.

Ken had been the bartender at Erin's Pub for

longer than John had been alive. He knew every sailor, captain and ship that had ever been in Oswego Harbor during his time. He also knew the comings and goings of them all better than the harbormaster did. It was no surprise at all to John that Ken knew about his orders less than ten minutes after he himself had found out. If you wanted to know anything that happened anywhere near the docks, Ken was the one to ask.

"Detroit is a two weeker right?"

"Sure is, well at least until we get those diesels installed. Why do you ask?"

"Oh no reason, just wanted to know how long your stool would be cold for that's all."

John smiled, but he knew from the bartender's tone that he was holding something back. He sat sipping at his whiskey for a few minutes and watching Ken wash glasses. He plopped the empty glass on the counter and looked out the window. It was getting a dark already and he thought he should be heading home.

"Can I get you another one?" Ken asked, still wiping glasses.

"Yeah, Ken one more will be fine. I've got to get home to Lindsey before too much longer, she's gonna want to see me for awhile before I go out. She gets lonely you know."

Ken looked John in the eyes as he said those last words, and then looked down at the glass as he poured in another dose of whiskey.

"That one is on me John," Ken said flatly as he turned to place the bottle back on the shelf.

"Oh that's not necessary Ken."

"No, it's no trouble," Ken rested both hands on the bar in front of John and leaned in closer to him.

"John I've known you since you were a kid and you've always been a great friend to me and my family," he paused and stared down at the varnished oak bar. Then he said, "What I have to tell you is about the hardest thing I think I've ever had to say to a friend."

"What is it Ken?" He had suspected that Ken was keeping something from him. But he hadn't expected anything all that serious. It seemed as though he'd been wrong.

"Well, do you know the Patton boy, Ryan?"

John frowned and said, "Yeah, he's that drunken little bastard who works on Healy's Farm down Fulton way."

"Yeah, well for about the last three months there have been rumors going round that every time a ship goes out on a run, Patton has been paying visits to a few of the sailors' wives. So I've been keeping my eyes open for awhile now, you know, watching out for you boys."

John's face began to turn red.

Ken cleared his throat and continued in a lower voice, "Well, I started hearing things about him and Lindsey. At first I didn't think nothing of it knowing her like I do and I didn't want to rile you up over nothing, so I didn't say nothing for awhile. But this last Friday, the night before you got back from Toronto I saw them together over on Sellman St. I was walking home after closing up here. It was around one in the morning and they were in the shadows next to Morrissey's Pharmacy and they were all over each other.

"Now, John you know I wouldn't say anything if I wasn't sure and you know that and it kills me inside to tell you, but you had to know."

After he finished he reached out and patted John on the shoulder and stepped away to give him some time to think.

John stared absently at the gleaming bar glass for a long time trying in vain to suppress the rage that was rising within him. A sickening knot tightened in his stomach over Lindsey's utter betrayal. He had wondered for some time about this very thing. But like Ken he thought there was no way his wife would do this to him; his sweet, caring wife. Another wave of anger rushed over him as that thought passed through his mind. His rage and sorrow were overwhelming.

He downed the rest of his whiskey and then stormed out of the pub. Ken went to the window and watched him disappear around the corner across the street.

"Poor boy," he said under his breath as he turned back to the bar to wait on his other patrons.

A group of Canadian sailors at the end of the bar were singing a song together in French. Ken painted on a smile and joined in and tried not to think about the pain John must be feeling or what it might mean for his future.

* * *

John and Lindsey Peters lived in a small cape style house on the shore of Lake Ontario just outside the village of Oswego. Shortly after leaving the pub he was sitting on a stone fence a few hundred yards from the house, staring blankly at their home through the now moonlit evening air. The wind that constantly beat the shoreline was drying the tears from John's cheeks almost as quickly as they flowed from his eyes.

He had watched Lindsey come out on the porch and holler to their son John Jr. to come in for dinner. He pictured them in his mind sitting down at the table. His boy, muddy from playing on the lake shore, would wash up while his mother set the table. The two would sit down and Lindsey would lie to God about thanks and loyalty as she had so often lied to him and their son. Johnny, oblivious to the storm that lay ahead of him would happily eat his dinner and wait for his dad to come home, while Lindsey would be waiting for morning when he would leave.

After an hour or so of sitting on the fence John had calmed himself enough to be able to maintain composure for his son's sake. So he made his way to the house, walking through the wet grass of the field that surrounded it.

He walked up the porch steps but before he reached the door it swung open and Johnny jumped in to his arms.

"Daddy!" the boy yelled with joy as John pulled his son to him and hugged him tight.

John's heart was a knot of mixed emotions. At once he felt joy and love for his son and blistering rage for his wife. The rage was magnified by the other emotion. He hated her for the damage she had done to his family. He began to sob as he held Johnny to him.

Johnny squeezed his dad tighter and said, "Daddy, what's wrong?"

In his nine years of life he had never before seen his father cry.

"Nothing son," John said setting the boy down and wiping his eyes, "what'd you have good for dinner?"

"Mommy made chowder," he said smiling and his eyes lit up as he emphasized the word "chowder".

John managed a smile at that. He put his hand on his son's shoulder as they walked into the house. Once they were inside Johnny ran upstairs to tell his mom that his dad was home and John went to the kitchen to find some of the soup.

He listened to his son's stomping feet as he ran upstairs and down the hall to his parents' bedroom. He heard the sound of muffled voices. Then after a few minutes two sets of footfalls came down the stairs much more slowly.

Lindsey came into the kitchen as John was sitting down with the lukewarm soup.

"Stop by Erin's on the way home?" she asked walking toward the wash basin to clean the supper dishes.

"Yeah," John answered sharply trying not to look at her.

"You head out in the morning, right?"

"Yeah, for Detroit, it's a two weeker," he said lifting the spoon to his mouth.

"Johnny misses you terrible when you're gone that long," she said over the clatter of the dishes.

"Yeah, I know Johnny does."

She stopped and turned to look at her husband. His tone had been sharp the entire time and she had tried to let it go. She figured he was just tired or worried about the trip. But this comment, with such bite to it meant something more and she knew it.

She said, "What is that supposed to mean?"

John finished the soup without another word. He dropped the spoon in the empty bowl. Then he got up from the table and went into the parlor with his son. Lindsey turned toward the sink, hiding her face in her hands and began to cry. She knew without any doubt that he knew about her mistake. She knew as soon as she did what she had done with Ryan that this day would come. She hadn't expected it to come so soon but she knew it was inevitable.

After taking a few minutes to compose herself Lindsey went to the parlor. There she found her son and husband playing checkers by the dormant fireplace. She stood in the doorway for a few minutes watching them. She had to choke back more tears as Johnny beamed with pride and puffed out his chest every time he said "king me" to his dad. John was his son's hero, watching them together for five minutes made that abundantly clear. Everything John was Johnny wanted to be, everything he did Johnny wanted to do. As long as his dad was around everything was okay. She knew that she was robbing her son of that security and her heart ached with guilt.

"Well, boys I'm turning in," she said in a thick voice. She walked over to the table where they were playing and put a hand on Johnny's head and said, "What do you say?"

Johnny slumped his shoulders and slid out of the chair in silent protest. He hugged his dad and went upstairs. John sat in silence staring at the checker board. Lindsey waited for him for a moment and when it was clear to her he wasn't coming she went upstairs without him.

An hour or so later he came into the bedroom. She felt the bed shift under his weight as he climbed in. Had she been sleeping it might have awoken her. He covered up and lay beside her in the silence for a few minutes.

"I think we should talk," Lindsey said.

"We have nothing to talk about," John said into the darkness above him.

"Johnny is going to stay with my brother for the week so he can help out at the lighthouse. While he is there I can make preparations to be gone when you get back from Detroit."

"I think the preparations have already been made."

"John, I am so sorry," she said as he rolled away from her.

The couple lay in silence sharing a bed for the last time. Outside the wind was blowing up a monster of a storm. In their bedroom one was already raging.

* * *

John awoke to the sound of a window shutter slamming against the side of the house. He arose from bed and went to the window. As he opened the pane a blast of rain dowsed him, washing away any chance at returning to sleep that he may still have had. He reattached the latch to the shutter and closed the window then went to prepare for his departure.

It was early, but he knew with the unexpected bad weather, getting to the dock as soon as he could was a good idea. Because of the storm this voyage just became twice as difficult as it would otherwise have been. The Great Lakes are very moody ladies. When the weather is less than perfect a sailor can never be too prepared to wrangle with them.

John went to his son's bedroom and kissed the boy on the forehead. Johnny woke up and threw his arms around his dad's neck and squeezed him tightly. John almost lost his balance but caught himself and hugged his son back.

"You leavin' dad?"

"I sure am and I'm gonna miss you kid."

"I'll miss you too daddy. Be careful and remember one hand for you and one for the ship," he said as he let go his grip and rested back on his pillow.

John smiled at his own words coming from the boy's mouth, "I will buddy, I promise and I'll see you in two weeks. I love you Johnny, more than anything."

"I love you too, daddy," Johnny said with a yawn as his dad mussed his hair and left the room.

John left the house and headed for the village well before sunrise and was serenaded by thunder and wind for most of the trip. When he reached the dock most of the crew was already on board the ship making final preparations and securing the cargo for departure. Within an hour everything was ready and they set sail early at around four thirty.

The ship steamed away from the dock and across the harbor toward the twenty foot crests that were now crashing against the break wall. The lighthouse on the end of the wall stood like a sentinel, its beam sliced through the dark rainy morning. As it always had it carried out its duty of warning sailors about the wall of boulders which it stood upon and showing the way to safe harbor. John thought how happy his son would be working with his uncle for the week. Lindsey's brother Ernest was the lighthouse keeper. He was a good man whose only sin in John's book was that of being Lindsey's brother. Johnny always loved going out to the light. His eyes would glow with excitement at every step across the wall whenever his dad and he would walk out to the point. It was a good place for the boy to be right now.

A little smile broke on John's face as the ship passed the tip of the wall and the huge white steel building with its fifty foot light tower protruding from the east side. But his smile quickly faded when the ship broke the point and he saw the waves that were hiding on the other side. Inside the break wall the crests were high, at around five feet but on the lake side they were massive, nearly the height of a two story house. John's appreciation for the wall was renewed when he saw the waves he would now have to ride.

The ship cut through the waves with no trouble for about twenty miles. The sun was just peeking over the horizon to the east, but black clouds were quickly jumping in front of it as it rose.

John looked at it muttering under his breath, "You lied to me big guy, thanks a lot."

The pilot kept the ship just off shore about a quarter mile out. The crew felt far more at ease being tossed around in the waves as long as the shore was visible again with each trough. Almost as quickly as they would catch site of the land again another swell would rise over the side of the ship, casting a deluge onto the deck.

The ship and crew continued this game of peek-a-boo with the shore for about an hour until the storm suddenly turned for the worse. Within an hour the wind had increased to almost sixty miles an hour and the swells had almost doubled in height. In his years on the lakes, John had seen many storms of this magnitude but he had never seen one progress this fast.

The waves were now hitting the ship in the bow rather than the starboard side as they had been for much of the trip. With each swell the ship would rise forty feet and then nose dive into the trough as the next wave crashed onto the bow deck. The captain decided to lay over in Rochester until the storm subsided a little. That is if they could make Rochester. Meanwhile, the waves and the rain continued to batter the ship.

The captain went to the radio console and picked up the microphone. He radioed the Rochester harbormaster about the situation and advised him they were bringing the ship in with an estimated time of arrival of two hours. The reply from the Rochester was drowned out by a thunderous crash from inside the hull of the ship.

The engineer radioed the bridge to notify the captain that a large amount of the ships cargo of timber had broken free from its tension straps and slammed into a bulkhead near the bow in the hull of the ship. It had done a fare amount of damage but as of now there was no leaking.

As he gave his report the ship lifted up with another swell. As the bow dipped down a vicious rumble vibrated through the entire ship and as she crashed into the trough a loud ripping sound sliced through the storm from beneath the ship and the deck hatches. The frantic voice of the engineer again crackled through the bridge speakers, telling the crew what they already knew. The load had shifted as the ship slid down the last wave and crashed into the bulkhead, as the bulkhead caved in it had torn a massive hole in the port side of the ship.

She began to list almost immediately to port. The drag on that side of the ship shifted their trajectory towards the shore. The captain gave the order to abandon the ship over the loud speaker as the twenty men above decks began jumping into the lake.

John climbed down the stairs from the bridge deck and stepped onto the severely angled main deck. As the ship again began to rise up he grabbed onto the handrail. He squeezed the rail until his knuckles began to turn white as the ship again crashed down against the pit of water. Looking up he saw that shore was no more than a few hundred feet away. He couldn't tell where they were but shore was shore at this point. The trees and rocks were barely visible through the rain but he knew he could make it. He waited for one more cycle of waves as the ship was now at a sixty degree list. When she hit the trough again he jumped.

The cold water engulfed him as his weight and momentum brought him under. His descent bottomed out at about ten feet and he began to float back to the surface dodging sinking timber and chunks of steel as he ascended. He was aware of how the silence under water was such a stark contrast to the violent storm that raged above. As soon as air hit his lungs he swam as hard and fast as he could away from the ship. He could hear her behind him, as the waves pounded her metal hull and as she smashed into the trough of water every few minutes. The ship sounded like a giant steel slink worm chasing him across the surface of the lake as he swam for his life.

John swam hard for about fifteen minutes then paused for a moment to catch his breath and get his bearings. As he floated there amid the rain and the waves a deafening explosion suddenly tore through the storm. Instinctively he took a gulp of air and dove under water. Again the eerie silence engulfed him. He waited until his lungs burned for oxygen then forced himself to count to ten. The first feint black spots floated across his vision. When he could wait no longer for fear of passing out he finally allowed himself to float to the surface.

When he broke the surface he treaded water and took in his surroundings. He saw that he was very close to shore. Quickly he scanned the shoreline and then the water around him for some sign of his shipmates but all he saw was flaming debris. They are all excellent swimmers, he thought to himself. Surely if he could make it to shore he'd find them there. He refused to believe that he was the only survivor. But if he didn't make it to shore soon he wouldn't have to worry about that.

So he did the only thing he could do, he started swimming.

* * *

John pulled his exhausted body out of the water and onto the rocks. He propped himself up against a pine tree and sat for a moment watching the rain pound the surface of the lake. The din of the rainfall and the roar of waves were the only sounds he heard. Again he scanned the shore and the water, but there was no one there. No one at all had come out of the lake but him.

He sat until he thought he had enough strength to walk. Then he forced himself to stand up and he began moving east along the shoreline. He walked a little way into the woods away from the rocky shore and the driving rain. He walked until he began to tire again then he found a spot to rest.

He reached into his pocket and pulled out a chunk of jerky strips wrapped in wax paper. He lay on the ground chewing the jerky and thinking about what he should do. His wife was gone, his ship had sunk and his whole crew was dead. He had no one now. He thought to himself that no one even knew he was alive.

John sat up suddenly staring a thousand miles away into the forest as that thought boomed through his head.

"No one even knows I'm alive," he said aloud to himself.

John stood up, wrapped up the jerky and stuffed it in his pocket and began sprinting through the woods toward Oswego. His fatigue was forgotten. His realization filled him with a new energy.

He calculated in his head about how far he had to go. He knew from how long they'd been sailing before the ship sank and from an estimate of the actual speed they had been traveling, that he couldn't be much more than fifty miles from town. He decided to run until he either collapsed or the sun went down, which ever came first. He wanted to get as close to home as possible by the end of the day. His recent flood of grief had turned into an entirely different emotion all together now. This new emotion was far darker and sharp as the edge of a razor.

But with all he had been through his body gave up on him far quicker than he had hoped for. In less than two miles he simply collapsed under a pine tree and fell sound asleep. Emotional and physical exhaustion had caught up with him and there was no fighting it.

As he slept he dreamt of better days. Lindsey had been such a beautiful young woman. She had wavy blonde hair. When she smiled it outshined the sun. The love he'd felt for her back then was so powerful. It was the power of that love which was now fueling his pain. Even in dreams the sorrow crept in as the vision turned to a dark stormy night shortly after Johnny was born. John had come home one night from the docks to find Lindsey sprawled out on the parlor floor in their home. She had overdosed on tranquilizers and whiskey. She had sent Johnny to her mother's house while John was away. She hadn't realized he was only sailing up the shore to Mexico Bay and he'd be back the same night. He came in and found her naked and unconscious. He ran down the road to Dr. Marcum's house. The doctor returned with John and saved the woman and nothing was ever said of it after that. When John asked why she had done this she replied, "I wasn't ready for this." John wasn't sure at the time what she meant by that but yesterday he'd found out. If he had only known that night why he found her nude and why the doctor never said a word about it in town. If only he had realized at the time whom she had gotten the drugs from. But he still trusted her then. She was his loving new bride; they had just had a child. He had no idea what she really was and now that he did, he yearned to be ignorant once again. But, that was not possible.

* * *

The torrential rain had abated and was now a mere sprinkle and the gale force wind had dropped to a gentle breeze. The drops of rain falling on the leaves and under brush played a sort of symphony to the forest. A smoky colored squirrel scurried silently up the side of the pine tree that sheltered the sleeping man. It paused on a branch about half way up the tree to scan its surroundings before continuing on its journey. As it leapt from the tree the shaking branches released a shower of rainwater onto John's face waking him abruptly.

He sat up rubbing his eyes. It was still daylight and the sun had won most of its battle with the clouds but it was still obscured. The forest was silent except for the music of the rain. The lake, visible through the pines twenty feet away, had calmed dramatically but still tossed six foot crests toward heaven. John rose from the bed of pine needles and walked between the trees to the top of a bank by the lake. He looked west along the rocky shore, knowing he would see nothing of what he searched for. He had walked too far from the wreck to see anything of the ship and he knew that if any of the sailors had survived he'd have seen them by now. They would have either been on shore when he got there or they would have come across him in the woods as he slept since they would have undoubtedly headed for town as well. He was alone and he knew it; the lone survivor.

He lowered his head and walked down the shoreline to the east. As he walked his mind was clouded with all of the events of the last twenty four hours. His heart was heavy with visions of his wife in the arms of other men. It was heavier still at the thought of what his son would now have to endure. He was condemned to a separation from the normal life that children should rightfully know. His mind then shifted to his crew, friends that had endured so much with him. Friends now gone forever to the lake they had spent so much of their lives on. Irrational as it may be he blamed Lindsey for all of this and the more he thought about it the more intoxicated with rage he became at her.

He plodded on through the sprinkling rain formulating his plan. In his hyper-stressed and exhausted state his mind wasn't functioning clearly. His thoughts were murky and ill formed. The images from the past mixed with those he'd only imagined and all of those mixed with his plans for going forward until all of his thought was a big mixed up stew in which no individual thought was clear at all. None of his thoughts were clear that is except one. That one kept flashing in his mind like lightning on a stormy night. He had come to the conclusion that Lindsey would pay the price for all of his loss. She would pay in advance for all that Johnny was going to have to go through. John had decided that Lindsey was going to die tonight.

* * *

He reached the tree line at the western edge of town just before sunset. The rain had stopped completely. He sat on the edge of the woods watching the town breathe and waiting for the sun to bid farewell to the day. When darkness fell he cautiously made his way to the house where his wife had set all of this in motion. He crept along the road side, ducking into the underbrush at the most distant sight of headlights on the horizon, insuring that he would go undetected. He was dead as far as anyone knew and staying that way was the key to his future.

As he approached the house he could see that the lights were on in the parlor. He silently approached the window and peeked inside. Lindsey was sitting on the sofa with a box full of photographs on her lap. She thumbed through the box of memories pausing frequently to weep into the handkerchief that she clutched in her left hand. As he watched her his heart began to soften. He began to realize that she had at least some remorse and he almost changed his mind. But, again an image of her in the arms of Patton flashed before him. Then he thought of his son living without him and his sympathy for her melted away.

He stepped silently onto the porch and opened the door as quietly as possible to keep it from giving him away. The door opened into the kitchen which was at the back of the house. As he crept through the kitchen, walking as lightly as he could, he picked up a large candlestick holder from the table. He slunk down the hallway toward the parlor. He paused at the doorway and peeked into the room. Lindsey was sitting on the couch with her back to him completely unaware of his presence.

He paused for a moment leaning back against the wall. Tears ran down his face as he gripped the golden candlestick holder tightly in his hand. Then he took a deep breath and burst into the parlor holding it above his head. Lindsey heard the footfalls and as she turned to look John swung the golden club. It smashed against the side of her face so hard that the impact knocked it from his hand. Lindsey never knew what hit her. Her head whipped to the side from the force and her body flopped over onto the couch and then rolled lifelessly onto the floor.

John knelt down and retrieved his instrument of murder then walked over to his wife's body. He rolled her over and examined the damage he had done. The side of her face was crushed by the blow and blood oozed from the wound. He rolled her onto the area rug in front of the couch. He moved quickly so she wouldn't bleed on the floor any more than she already had. He removed the afghan from the back of the couch and spread it on the floor. He wiped up every speck of blood he could find with it. Then he rolled it and the body up in the rug. He performed a hasty but passable clean up job then he slung the grisly package over his shoulder and carried the candle holder in his hand and left the house.

Making it to the break wall this time of day undetected wouldn't be very difficult. The town rolled up the streets every night at seven o'clock and it was near ten now. It also helped that his house was on the shore not more than five hundred feet from the wall.

The rain had begun to fall again and the wind was picking up as well. John was a strong man having spent his life working as a sailor. Carrying the one hundred-ten pound body of his dead wife was no trouble for him. The blowing rain however was beginning to impede his travel some. He stumbled over a rock on the shore and nearly dropped his cargo twice before he made it to the wall. But he did make it eventually.

Upon reaching the granite wall he stopped to rest for a moment and laid the lifeless woman on the ground. He could see the rotating lamp atop the lighthouse at the other end of the wall. It cut through the five hundred feet of rain between him and it effortlessly. He surveyed the dark silhouetted hulk that stretched out in front of him. He saw no one on the wall or along the shore. His only concern was Ernest the lighthouse master and his own son who were out there in the lighthouse at the end of the wall. But, he knew that in rain like this he would be safe from their sight as long as he stayed low.

Once again he lifted the corpse onto his shoulder then he stepped onto the first granite slab. He knew he'd have to get at least a few hundred feet beyond the bend in the wall or the lake's depth would be insufficient to hide his evidence. So he set out walking through the rain atop the six foot wide granite wall out into Oswego Harbor with his wife's dead body on his shoulder.

    The breakwall in good weather and calm water has an apex above the lake's surface of about ten feet. That night the waves were high enough at times to break over the wall and douse the top of it with a heavy spray making them as slippery as ice. The lack of traction along with the darkness made traversing the wall very dangerous. The shape and structure of the rocks themselves added even more difficulty to the chore. When the stones were placed during the construction of the wall they weren't set in place very precisely. There are large gaps between them in some places and some of the gaps are as wide as two feet. John remembered slipping on the wet rocks when he was a boy and falling into one of them and breaking his arm. He could ill afford such an accident now.

    He reached a spot about half way between the elbow in the wall and the lighthouse where he stopped. He laid the bundled body on the rocks and removed it from its wrappings. Then he picked up his dead wife and held her in his arms. Her silk night gown flapped in the wind and clung to the wet skin. John was startled when goose bumps formed on her arms. He quickly checked her pulse thinking that maybe he hadn't really killed her after all but he found none. Then he knelt with her in his arms and spoke to his bride.

"I'm sorry it had to come to this Lindsey. I loved you more than anything in the world."

Then he kissed her cold lips and stood up. He looked up at the sky with the wind and rain pelting his face and tears streaming from his eyes. Then with all of his strength he tossed the body into the lake. He watched it rise and fall with the waves for a few minutes. He then dried his eyes and tightly wrapped the candlestick and the afghan into the rug and threw it all as hard as he could out into the water with Lindsey. Then he walked back across the wall to shore.

* * *

When he finished telling the story the old man took a final pull from his cigar and crushed it out on the rocks. The boys had been gripped by the tale and now sat mulling over the new information. It was Bobby who spoke up first.

"So what did he do next?"

"Well," the old man said, "When he reached shore he knew he would have to be out of the area well before dawn. He was well known in all of the coastal towns and his cover would quickly be gone. He couldn't take a ship obviously so he made his way to the rail yard.

"The rail yard was dark and the rain pounding on the boxcars made enough noise to cover any sound he might have made. He found a car from a Canadian shipping company and slid back the door. He called out into the dark interior of the boxcar to make certain he was alone. Back then train hopping was pretty common and some fairly dangerous people took to the practice. There were also the bulls to consider. They were folks hired by the railroads to discourage the stowaways. We'll just leave it at that. Once he was sure the car was vacant he climbed in and slid the door shut. He balled up his jacket and laid his head on it then he fell asleep sobbing. Those were the last tears he ever let himself cry over the affair. The next morning he woke up in Montreal then he headed west to begin a new life. Simple as that."

"Wow, did he ever see his son again?" Bobby

asked.

"A few years after the murder John sent a confidant he'd met in Canada back to town to see about the boy. He found John Jr. living with his uncle and doing alright in spite of all of the tragedy. The next year John returned himself. Under the cover of night he went out to the lighthouse and made contact with his son. He knew he was risking his life but he ached for the boy and he could no longer bear to go on without him. To his surprise it seemed as if Johnny had been waiting for him to come back. He thought that everyone assumed he was dead but Johnny thought no such thing.

"When Johnny asked why he had gone away his dad told him that he and his mom had a falling out. And even though it tore him up inside to do it he saw no other way at the time to keep peace in Johnny's life. But when he'd heard of Lindsey's suicide he came back to check on him. He felt it best that Johnny should grow up with Ernest at the lighthouse rather than be toted around the world by his sailor father. The lie was thin and they both knew it. But they missed each other so much that this fabrication passed as their truth for many years. Sometimes it is much easier to live with a lie than to face the truth.

"From then on every summer John would sail into Oswego Harbor and meet Johnny at the pier and they would go sailing for one week. This was all he could safely risk. But it was enough. It allowed Johnny to grow up knowing his father."

"You said the Lady disappeared because she found what she was looking for. What do you mean?" Randy asked.

"One summer day when the two men were out on their yearly trip another gale blew up. I say men because Johnny was fully grown by now of course. They were a mile out in a small sailboat when the wind and rain began hitting the boat hard. They steered for shore but their visibility was next to nothing. This wasn't long ago and it was years after the lighthouse had been converted to the automated solar powered contraption it is now. But at that particular time it was out of service as it seems to be three or four times a year these days. The boat had no radar and they were coming into Oswego blind. As they struggled to see the wall they suddenly beheld a golden light that sliced through the rain. As they sailed closer to it the two men saw a sight that shocked them to their souls. It was the ghost of Lindsey carrying her golden candle atop the break wall. The strange glow lit the way for them through the gale all the way to the pier."

"She saved them." Carl whispered.

"She did. I believe that she atoned for what she had done and forgave John for what he had done in that one act of grace," said the old man.

The boys went silent for awhile. Then Bobby asked the man shyly, "How do you know all this?"

The old man looked at Bobby and said, "The real story of the Lady of the Wall was only known by two people. Those two people were John Peters and me. John knew because he was the man with the torn soul. The man who had enough anger in his heart to lead him into a realm of evil he would never have considered under normal circumstances. And I know because I was there.

"The thud of the gold against Lindsey's head may have been a dull sound but the sound of her body rolling onto the hardwood floor was loud. Loud enough to wake a nine year old boy from a sound sleep in his bedroom upstairs. My mother was going to bring me to the lighthouse to work with my uncle for the week but she changed her mind after she got word that the ship had disappeared and instead she kept me at home.

"I awoke to what I thought was the sound of the

woodpile tipping over in the parlor. I went to the stairs to see if my mother was alright. As I reached the top of the stairs I saw my father rolling her onto the rug by the couch. The side of her face was bloody and her head was concave. My excitement at seeing that my father had survived the wreck faded quickly when I realized what had happened in our parlor. I sat at the top of the stairs watching him wrap her up and carry her out. I was heartbroken over what I'd seen. I thought I would never see either of my parents again after that. I wanted to run to him and hug him and turn back the clock to before this had happened. I wanted to understand what had happened but understanding wouldn't come to me for along time.

"The next day when they found my mother's body on the shore I said nothing. I was sent to live with my uncle at the lighthouse where I worked my entire life until it was shut down on us many years later. In the months following her death many of my mothers secrets became common knowledge and the town's grief over the loss of my father far exceeded their grief at losing her.

"Many years after my father first sought me out he finally told me the truth about that night. I can only imagine how difficult it must have been for him to tell me that story. But I can also imagine it was a relief too. I was full grown by then and I knew far too much about the events surrounding that night to chasten him for a sin so long in the past; no matter how awful it was or how much it had affected our lives. I never told him what I'd seen that night. I saw no reason to add that to his already immense load of guilt. If it were up to me I'd say he had paid the price by carrying that guilt around for his entire life. But I know that it isn't up to me. Still, I have since realized that he was a good man and that what he'd done was not a true display of his character. The man I knew him to be was what he really was. I know now that I made the right choice in staying silent all these years. Now that he is gone I can tell his secret, now that he is safe. I feel better letting God judge him in death than I would have letting the people of this town judge him and take away what was left of his life. My heart is forever weighted over the loss of my parents and the loss of my happy childhood. But, now after all these years I guess I can understand both of them. More importantly, I can forgive both of them and now I can share the true story."

The boys were in awe of all of this new information. The real life son of the Lady of the Wall was sitting right in front of them. They could hardly believe it. But they did believe it. The five sat in silence for some time after the man's final words were spoken.

After awhile it started getting late and the boys set out for home, each of them bid goodnight to the old man as they left. He stayed a long time after they'd gone. He sat on the wall lost in his memories for most of the evening. When he finally stood to leave it was long after dark. He slowly walked the length of the break wall back to shore leaving behind the past and all of the sorrow that goes with it. He didn't look back to see the faint forms of his parents standing where he had left them, but somehow he knew they were there. As he left the wall for the last time he was smiling.

Jason R. LaPoint
August 4, 2004
Glens Falls, NY

OR- B.
(Operating Room-B)

I don't blame you at all if you don't believe me. I wouldn't believe it myself if I hadn't been there to see it. It's like one of those supermarket tabloid headlines, the kind you read and roll your eyes at how ridiculous they are. But unlike "Eiffel Tower Eaten by Termites" or "Lisa Marie Marries Batboy" this story actually happened and I know because I was there.

Christmas Day, 2004- Elk Valley Hospital, Elk Valley, PA.

I have always hated working holidays at the hospital. It never fails, we won't do a damn thing all day and then an hour before the shift is over something off the wall will happen. I have never worked a Christmas when my shift didn't either start or end with me in the morgue doing c-spine films on someone who got creamed in a car accident, or skull films on someone celebrating the holidays the old fashioned way, that is with their toe wrapped around a shotgun trigger. But what happened this year wasn't anything so common. This year what happened wasn't common at all.

The thing about being an x-ray tech is that we are needed all over the hospital not just in the department. We work in the OR, the ER, and the damned morgue and on occasion we even do films in patients' rooms. That is how I was able to see most of Margaret Hanlon's story first hand.

She came into the ER by rescue squad at a little after noon. She had apparently taken a nasty spill on the ice in front of her house. The ER called over and said they needed a hip and ankle on her. So I went over and shot the films and both exams were positive for fracture. The hip was pretty bad and that meant emergency surgery. Due to her age the on call surgeon, Dr. McCarran, decided to do both fractures at once. Naturally when the OR called saying they were ready for X-Ray, the tech who was assigned to go up was on lunch. So I was elected to do the procedure. I remember thinking how lucky I was. Now I would get to stay late on Christmas Day to do a three hour surgery that probably wouldn't even start until an hour before I was supposed to get out, joy to the freaking world.

As I walked through the ER toward the elevator I passed Margaret's room. Margaret's neighbor had ridden in with her and she was telling the nurse that Margaret had been behaving strangely when she fell. She described her bolting out of her front door and into the street screaming "GET IT OFF ME, GET IT OFF ME!" The neighbor said she'd gone out to help but by the time she got outside Margaret had already fallen on the ice.

I had become so accustomed to hearing this type of story in the ER that I paid little attention. But later the neighbor's words would resonate with me in a big way. After what happened in the OR that story would haunt me as much as anything that happened during the surgery. I still spend many nights unable to sleep at the thought of what may have caused Margaret to run in terror from her home.

The routine of setting up an OR suite is second nature for those of us who do it regularly and it went quickly. It was waiting for the on-call surgeon to arrive that took so much time. The ER called him when Margaret first came in and he had decided to do surgery right away.

So naturally two hours later he still wasn't there. I have no doubt he was at home getting outside of his fair share of figgy-pudding before he came in. Never mind the injured woman and five person staff who were in the OR waiting for him. Finally he arrived at 2:38 PM and we got started.

Dr. Morrison the anesthesiologist put Margaret under and the nurses began to sterilize the ankle first while McCarran scrubbed. When he came into the room the circulating nurse called a "time out", which is standard operating procedure. It's the way we make sure we're doing the right thing to the right part of the right person.

Morrison answered her, "Today's contestant is Margaret Hanlon. This seventy eight year old from Latrobe Pennsylvania has won herself a right ankle ORIF and a left hip ORIF."

Satisfied with the accuracy of the information McCarran nodded and we got under way. The procedure on the ankle went well and was uneventful. Dr. McCarran used a small metal plate and five screws to repair the broken fibula and one screw to secure the fibula to the tibia to sturdy the ankle up some more. I did my usual before and after pictures and the doctor closed after about forty-five minutes of surgery.

After the ankle was complete the nurses had to prepare the hip which meant McCarran and I had time to step out for a breather.

As we left the OR suite he removed his mask and sighed. "Were you down stairs when she came in," he asked me as he leaned on the scrub sink and rubbed the bridge of his nose.

"Yeah, I did your pre-op shots when she first came in around noon. How was dinner?"

"Ham was dry, potatoes were cold, you know how it is. Sorry I was late. The ER doc said she fell in the street. What's the scoop?"

"I didn't get much more than that myself. The neighbor brought her in. She said something about Mrs. Hanlon running out of her house screaming 'Get it off me!'"

"Get what off her?"

I shrugged and put my mask back on. "Don't know," I said as I pushed the door open and went back into the suite.

The scrub-nurse was waiting to re-gown Dr. McCarran when I entered. He scrubbed again then butted the door open. He held his arms out in front of him dripping water as he reentered.

"We found two small puncture wounds in her inguinal region on the left side when we prepped the hip doctor," she said handing him a sterile towel to dry his hands.

"Looks like whatever was on her had teeth," he said as he examined the wounds in her betadine stained skin.

"I'll note it on the chart and we'll treat it when we get her to PACU," the nurse said.

Doctor Morrison peered over the patient to look at the wound, "They almost look like bite marks don't they?"

"You think we've got vampires that go for the crotch instead of the neck," I said getting a unanimous chuckle from the crew.

"Must be a French vampire," McCarran said to another round of chuckles, "Alright lets get this over with."

He and the scrub-nurse draped the patient and he made his incision. He had just poked his finger into the incision to palpate the greater trochanter when he suddenly yanked his finger out of the cut.

"What the hell was that," he said aloud but to himself.

The moment he said it we all saw what he had felt. The entire surgical team watched in awe as a small white ball slowly emerged from the pink tissue of the thigh and dropped out of the incision onto the floor at McCarran's feet. He backed up instinctively so it wouldn't contaminate the sterile front of his body. Within a minute the sterile field would no longer matter.

The ball hadn't shown up on my scout films so it had to be soft but it looked a lot like a marble. It was the purest white I have ever seen and glassy. No blood or tissue stuck to it at all. It was a perfectly clean little orb.

We all looked at it for a moment in silence. Then a low hum began to fill the room. Perhaps it was the orb itself I can't be sure. It was hardly perceptible at first but it quickly magnified in volume until it was like the hum of the engines on a jet. The telemetry screens and my C-Arm monitor went crazy with static and the overhead lights flickered. As we watched the little orb cracked around its equator and began to grow into an oblong shape like a glass tampon applicator. All the while the hum steadily intensified until the room itself began to vibrate. Stainless steel surgical instruments rattled together and some fell on the floor. All at once the glass tampon thing exploded in a puff of green vapor which quickly filled the room. The stuff was thick and noxious and it smelled like a dirty diaper, long forgotten in the trunk of a car in summer time.

In unison the screen on my monitor, the telemetry screens and the lights all burst. When they did sparks flew through the rancid green haze. The nurses tried for the door but they couldn't budge it.

In a matter of seconds the green cloud began to drop forming a putrid fog. The room was now lit only by light shining in from the hallway through the frosted windows. What I saw in the dim light made the most horrible thing I had ever seen before that moment pale in comparison to it. In the middle of the room where the glass tampon had been stood a beast like none I had ever seen. It was over six feet tall with large translucent wings. It had red skin which was covered with some kind of black exoskeleton. Its feet and hands were huge and each ended in large golden talons. The head was as much bird-like as it was lizard-like and its eyes were like murky light green balls of wax that seamed to glare at us. Its large beak-like mouth dripped clear drool and it bared its inch long yellow teeth at us in a demonic grin.

Dr. Morrison stood at the head of the patient with the beast between us and him. He tried to back away from the creature and accidentally kicked the stool he had been sitting on during surgery. At the sound the thing turned sharply and loomed over him completely eclipsing him from our view. With one swipe of its meaty right arm it sliced Morrison into four pieces with its golden talons.

As it turned back to face us it looked at Mrs. Hanlon lying on the table sedated and helpless. It cocked its head to the right and licked its teeth in a slow deliberate manner that sent chills down my spine. It reached under her and lifted her above its head. She hung in the air with the beast's talons stabbing into her at the pelvis and shoulders. It held her there above the OR table either dead or well on the way. Her body was arched and her IV line dangled from her hand. The creature opened its maw. It looked up at her and screeched through its bear trap mouth. It shoved the woman in and devoured her whole with gruesome indifference. Its powerful jaws snapped her bones and gouts of blood drooled out of its mouth as it chewed. Its maw moved side to side like a cow chewing cud.

After its meal it turned slowly and menacingly back to face the rest of us. We were now huddled by the useless exit door which was being held shut by some unseen force. The beast began to move toward us and I grabbed the closest heavy object I could find, which ended up being the fire extinguisher. I attacked it with repeated blows to its midsection and head which accomplished little more than to piss it off. But at least I was diverting its attention away from the others. As I fought the creature dodging the repeated swipes of its talons McCarran had the idea that would end up saving the rest of our lives.

He moved behind the shattered C-Arm monitor and he pushed the heavy machine into the creature sharply knocking it to the floor. As it lay there stunned I opened up with the extinguisher. I sprayed its face relentlessly as McCarran grabbed an IV pole and separated it from its base. He held the pole by his ear like a javelin and thrust it into the creature over and over. It shrieked an awful mechanical sounding scream. It wailed like that for what seamed like an eternity then finally the creature let out a throaty moan and was still.

In an instant the hum returned only it was far more intense this time. The room began to vibrate as it would in an earthquake. Dust fell from the ceiling and the doors shook in there frames. Then as abruptly as it had begun it stopped.

The beast lay on the floor covered in white flame retardant chemicals. The IV pole protruded from its lifeless chest. Around the beast the OR suite was utter devastation. Broken equipment and that green haze, which had now accumulated on the floor like rancid snow, was everywhere. Dr. Morrison's body lay in pieces along the back wall in a pool of blood. The rest of the survivors and I stood speechless amid the destruction. Then the body of the beast began to melt like ice. We watched as it slowly began to liquefy until at last it was completely gone like a forgotten nightmare that leaves behind only a feeling of unattached fear in its wake.

One of the nurses tried the door again and this time it opened as it always had. We exited the demolished OR suite to find a hallway full of OR staff all with the same shocked and questioning stares. But we had no answers. It happened so fast and it was so bizarre that any question we might try to answer could only be met by more questions.

The hospital reported it as a fire. The official report said the fire had begun with an explosion in the anesthesia machine. Despite the valiant efforts of the OR team, whose brave actions had saved the hospital and countless lives, the patient in surgery and one doctor were killed in the disaster. It's just as well that they lied. No one in their right mind would believe the truth anyway. I'm not even sure if the hospital's investigative team believed us. But I am sure now just why Margaret was screaming as she ran from her house that Christmas Day. She had undoubtedly been visited by one of those things. A pregnant beast from hell, or space or God knows where, who was looking for an incubator. Well it found one and I can only imagine what her terror must have been like. As frightened as we were that day in O.R.-B at least we weren't alone with the beast like she had been.

Jason LaPoint
September 1, 2005
Saratoga Springs, NY

The Tenacious Nature of Bees

Hundley lumbered out to the barn cussing at the cold and his own aching limbs all the while. He couldn't remember the days when his knees cooperated before sunrise. Now the long bones of his legs felt like brittle sticks of glass that were slowly crumbling at the ends even on warm days. And this was no warm day. This was one of those balmy November mornings that made him wonder why the hell he hadn't moved to Florida like every other 80 year old New Yorker who had any sense at all. But the snow-bird thing never seemed right for him. So here he was, up before the sun and freezing his withered old pills off for no good reason. Every winter that he endured only made him angrier. But that was the story of Hundley's life; impotent anger. He spat an improbable accusation at the rooster as he shuffled past him to vent his ire.

The tired old hinges on the barn door creaked loudly as he swung it open. He thought that was what his joints would sound like if he could hear them. He flipped on the light in the tack room. The light buzzed to life slowly in protest against the cold. Nothing liked waking up on mornings like this. He crossed the dirt floor to the grain bin. He grunted as he lifted the old broken cinder block from the lid. He had to weight it down or the God damned rats got into the feed. At least the vermin had some gumption in the wintertime. He set the block aside and pushed up the lid. He dipped one twisted claw-like hand into the cold dry corn feed and took out a handful. He dumped it into a plastic freezer bag and repeated the process three or four times until the bag felt full enough to him. Then he stuffed the baggie into his hip pack and replaced the lid and block. He flicked off the light and slammed the door shut then he headed off across the yard.

It was still an hour before sunup. The barnyard and the field beyond were still cast in the light of the moon. Everything was black and white, the way it should be. Beyond the yard was the field and beyond the field loomed the hulking black form of Sugar Mountain. Hundley plodded on through the darkness into the field. It was colder in the field than it had been in the yard and it had been plenty cold enough there. Once he was in the field his progress was slowed by the ankle deep snow and the frozen fronds of goldenrod that grew thick across most of the expanse. Hundley envied the plants; he wished that he too could simply lay dormant through the brutal cold of winter. But he couldn't so he cursed the goldenrod too.

The frozen snow crunched beneath his feet as he trudged on. He came to a stone fence on the far side of the field. The fence formed the border of an old apple orchard which lay at the foot of the mountain. The orchard like the rest of the farm had been neglected for a long time and it was overgrown with sumac and still more goldenrod. But the apples still popped out every fall just the same. Hundley followed the wall until he came to a place where the stones had been knocked away over time creating a low spot where he could step over it with relative ease. The floor of the orchard was littered with deer tracks, so much so that the snow was mashed into a muddy pulp in most places. The runs flowed this way and that among the stumpy apple trees and scattered undergrowth. Hundley picked a path that seemed to go in the right direction and followed it. This made the going easier for awhile. Some gracious doe had done him the trouble of clearing a path and the mud was still frozen enough so even that wouldn't hinder his pace much. But the crossing of the orchard would be the end of his easy travel. The face of Sugar Mountain was to follow.

He stepped over the opposite wall of the orchard and stood looking up at the darkened monolith and cursed the slope, the cold and the early hour. Then he set off up the mountain.

The snow was much thinner among the trees. The ground was covered with fallen leaves and twigs which lay amid the trunks and blow-downs. Everything was frozen and still. In all of that stillness the sound of his footfalls on the dried leaves sounded like a cacophony but Hundley had long ago given up trying to walk quietly through the woods.

One day when he was a teenager he and his father went out hunting. They were doing a drive through the woods near the eastern slope of the mountain. His father and he started out about a quarter of a mile apart and walked toward each other in the hope that one of them might jump a deer to the other. The point of a drive is not to be quiet in fact it's quite the opposite. The object is actually to try to startle the deer and get them to run at the other hunter. But Hundley couldn't help himself. He had it in his head that he had to sneak through the woods while he was hunting at all times and once he had something in his head, nothing including his own logic could make him do anything to the contrary. But this particular time would be a watershed moment.

He was paying so much attention to silencing his footsteps that he wasn't paying enough attention to where he was placing them. He stepped a little too hard on what he thought was a stone but was actually a rotted chunk of log. The log gave way under his weight and he staggered which would have been alright had he not been walking along a ledge. He pitched awkwardly out over the reach and before he knew it he was falling headlong through the brush down a steep hillside. He tumbled and bounced nearly forty feet before coming to rest on his rear end in a small streamlet.

For a moment he just sat there assessing what if

any damage he had done to himself. When he was certain he had no broken bones he gathered himself and looked back up the hill that he had just fallen down. It was nothing short of a miracle that he was alive after the fall, much less uninjured. He took a deep breath and for one of the few times in his life he turned his eyes skyward and said thank You.

When he lowered his eyes back to his surroundings he was shocked to see an eight point buck staring at him from less than twenty yards away. He couldn't have made more noise falling down the hill if he had tried to. But nevertheless there stood the deer watching the entire fiasco unfold.

Hundley fumbled for his rifle and shot the poor damned thing before it ever knew what happened. That episode cured him of any notion he'd ever had about the value of trying to be a silent hunter.

Not that he much cared about scoring deer anymore anyway. The days of pining over a prize rack had long since passed for old Hundley. In fact he didn't even like the meat anymore. Venison gave him the shits something awful and that is a dangerous affliction for an octogenarian to have. In truth Hundley wasn't sure why he still felt compelled to trudge his weary bones out here every fall at all. Maybe it was some kind of inner calling. But he thought not. It was more likely that it was just a habit like letting the phone ring twice before picking up. It was just something he'd always done so he just kept on doing it. But, whatever the reason, here he was again; brittle bones, bad eyes and all.

He wove his way through the hardwood along the slope of the mountain's base. It was still dark and the moonlight barely penetrated here at all so the progress was slow. It was a good thing the incline wasn't very steep yet. He had to pay very close attention to his footing in the dark. The operation would be even more difficult if the grade was more aggressive. Thank God for small favors. After awhile the hardwood gave way to a more easily passable stretch of pine. This section of woods was old so the trees were bigger and more spread out. Here he could see the sky through the canopy with ease. It was a black dome specked with twinkling lights. Some people believe that when the sun sets at the end of the day the spirit of it becomes a new star and that all of those little sparkling lights are a record of each individual day that has ever been. But Hundley had little use for such philosophical nonsense. To him the clear sky simply meant more cold and he couldn't wait for the sun to come up to throw a little heat on the subject.

The slope was indeed becoming steeper now and he was laboring quite a bit against it. Every so often he would stop to lean on a tree or a boulder to catch his breath all the while cursing this fool's errand. But finally he reached his destination.

Up ahead in the moonlight he could see the forest part and the land level off. A large clearing about the size of a baseball field stretched out before him. It was covered with wispy green grass and intermittently little tufts of foxgloves and milkweed which sprang up here and there through the frozen snow. In the center of the field stood a gnarled old pear tree that had no logical business being there at all. Even more of a mystery is how the thing could continue to produce fruit. God only knows how far away the nearest other pear tree is for the thing to pollinate with. But there it was and as always it hung heavy with fruit. Hundley never gave the enigma much thought. He just chalked the whole thing up to the tenacious nature of bees. Mysteries never interested him much. In truth nothing at all interested him very much these days.

Hundley crunched across the open meadow until he came to the peculiar pear tree. Then he unzipped his hip pouch and tugged the baggie out. He poured the dry corn in a neat little mound under the tree then crumpled the empty bag up and stuffed it back in the pouch. That done he simply stood there staring blankly at his work for some time. He stood so perfectly still that the scene could just as easily have been a painting rather than a real man in a real field. He could have been the subject of some bizarre vision in the mind of Andrew Wyeth. These episodes were becoming quite frequent for Hundley, several times a day for several minutes at a time his mind would simply slip out of gear and leave him standing stock still staring at a wall or a window or a pear tree. Then after a bit he would come around usually with no idea that anything had happened at all, which is what happened then. He stood for a good five minutes staring blankly at the little tree then as if no time had passed at all he simply zipped his pouch and walked off across the meadow.

    He came to a stone wall on the far side of the clearing and followed it. Sugar Mountain is covered with a web of these stone walls. Their source is no mystery, generations ago all of this forest was clear cut for lumber and the remaining fields were used as farm land. The stones were plucked from the fields to save damage to the plows and stacked into fences. But the odd thing was their positioning. It made no logical sense at all. Not one of the walls marked any property line that Hundley ever knew of and he had lived on Sugar his entire life. They also didn't delineate any field borders or at least not any that were readily apparent. As far as Hundley could tell they were just randomly constructed at the whim of some compulsive stone mason with nothing better to do. But as with the mystery of the pear tree and his own hunting habit, Hundley could not have cared less. Maybe people just do weird habitual things on Sugar Mountain.

Near the center of this particular stretch of wall a large maple tree had budged its way through the stones long ago and nestled in as if it were a part of the construction. Hundley reached the tree and looked up. Among the branches about twenty feet up he could see the shadowy shape of the tree-stand he had built there many decades before. Leaning against the tree was a treacherous old ladder that was newer than the stand but not by a lot. Hundley sighed then he wrapped a hand around one of the rungs and started climbing. The thought of the ladder collapsing and killing him never crossed his mind though it probably should have. It creaked and groaned under his weight protesting the load.

When he finally reached the tree-stand he was exhausted. His muscles felt like they were on fire and his knees and hips were equally enraged. He leaned his rifle against the tree and dropped his hip pack to the floor and then collapsed on the old pine bench. For a minute he just sat there with his eyes closed and rested his weary body. Then he pulled off a glove and rubbed the bridge of his nose with one gnarled old paw.

"Hunting over a bait pile isn't exactly ethical you know," said a voice off to his left.

Hundley didn't react at all. There was no startled jump, no gasp, nothing, he just kept massaging his nose and resting. After a moment he scowled and said, "Garrett. Aren't you dead?"

Garrett frowned. "Now is that any way to greet an old friend?"

"Friend my ass and what the hell have you ever known about ethics?"

Hundley unzipped his rifle case and pulled out his old .30-30. He ran his thumb over the stamp on the barrel which read Winchester Model 94 30-30 WIN made in New Haven, Conn. USA Winchester Proof Steel. He felt the stamped letters under the pad of his thumb, the old familiar feel of it comforted him. He always rubbed the stamp before shoving five shells through the little door on the side of the action. Putting in five shells was just another habit. Then he deliberately chambered a round while eyeing Garrett menacingly.

"Are you going to come here every year until I croak just to torment me, is that it?"

Garrett looked at him in disbelief. Then he looked down at the gun and raised his eyebrows.

"It is very interesting that you should put it just that way. The things you don't see are alarming to me Hundley, you know that? Speaking of, would you mind pointing that gun somewhere else? Your record with hunter safety isn't exactly sparkling you know."

He nodded at the gun and arched his brows again. Hundley just grunted and turned the gun and his eyes to the meadow below. The first tendrils of daylight were just beginning to creep into the sky.

Hundley chose to ignore most of what Garrett had said as usual.

"Shit, it ain't like it'd do any harm to you anyway even if I emptied this pepper mill into your rotting guts."

"Spoken like a true gentleman as always. Tell me

old friend, how is the business these days?" Garrett asked, changing the subject.

"Business is fine. Better'n it ever was."

"Oh, somehow I doubt that," Garrett said.

"What do you know?"

"I know that if I hadn't loaned you the start up money you'd have never been in business to begin with and I also know that my little event relieved you of the tiresome burden of having to pay me back. That's convenient, eh?"

Hundley squinched his face as if he had just bit into a lemon but he said nothing.

Garrett went on, "It reminds me of that time in France. You remember the time I mean, old pal? You do don't you?"

Still Hundley stared off at the meadow and said nothing. He was trying to ignore the other man but his expression and the color rising in his cheeks betrayed him.

"Cat got your tongue old boy?"

"Go fuck yourself Garrett."

"Oh come on. Take a walk down memory lane with me old buddy."

"I ain't your buddy and I ain't walking nowhere and I don't give two shits about France."

"Boy that has to have been, what, sixty years ago or so now, right? I honestly don't know. Time is kind of funny on this side of the curtain. But it's been awhile I know that. I mean hell, I was alive then," he said matter-of-factly.

"Hmph," Hundley said.

"Well I'll tell you what I remember, I remember you lying in a bomb crater with a big old meaty hole in your guts," Garrett said, and then he laughed as if he was telling about the time he caught Hundley peaking at old Jane Holloway's panties. "That was a rip remember? Side splitting you might say."

Hundley looked sideways at him and shook his head but said nothing.

"But the best part was when I picked you up and carried you out of no man's land on my shoulders while old Adolph's lead was tearing through the leaves all around us. Boy those were good times; a nice quality way to spend my short time on Earth."

"What do you want, a fucking medal? Oh, right they gave you one. Now get over it."

Garrett chuckled humorlessly. "Ah medals," was all he said and then his mind trailed off for awhile.

For a few minutes the two men just sat looking out at the rising day and thinking back to a long gone time and a far away place. What had they been in that forest for anyway? What was it that was worth killing and almost dying for? It seemed so long ago and all of the reasons seem so cloudy and vague now. The urgency of those days has been lost in the cloud of time.

"I do so cherish that medal," Garret said after a time. "I got a medal you got your life, seems fair to me."

"Quit your bitching, Garrett. We both came home. Nothing happened to you over there. I'm the one got ripped open and pissed blood for two years." It could have been the sunrise playing tricks on the eye but Hundley's face seemed to be getting redder by the minute and when he spoke the veins on his neck seemed to bulge out precariously.

"Yes, well, war is hell, or so I've heard," Garrett said mockingly. "But we did come home and we do have our memories, like the one of you starting your business and also the one of our little hunting trip."

At that Hundley flinched as if he'd been stung. But

he quickly tried to hide his reaction by shifting on the bench. He picked up the rifle and pointed it at something off across the field and then shook his head and lowered it again. Then he resumed his gaze at the meadow. In spite of all of his fidgeting, or perhaps because of it, it was clear that Garrett had gotten Hundley riled up and that his last point had touched a nerve more than the talk of war and money ever had.

"What happened was an accident and we both know it," Hundley said after some time.

"Do we?"

Hundley shot him a sideways glance and said, "We do."

Garrett looked away and said, "Well, all I know is you brought me up here hunting one time and I've been here ever since. While you have been out there ruining your business, clogging your arteries and expanding your surgically repaired gut I've been up here on Old Sugar, whiling away the hours conferring with the flowers."

"Ah hell, that was years ago. I can't believe you're still mad about it."

Garrett looked at him in awe. "Really? You can't believe I'd still be mad that you killed me? You are some kind of special, Hundley."

"I told you it was an accident damn it. I didn't kill you."

Garrett said nothing for a long time; he simply let the silence run on. A chipmunk rustled in some leaves off to their right. Hundley wasn't fooled by the sound. That is if he'd heard the sound at all. His mind was preoccupied by thoughts of a cold day much like this one six decades in the past.

That day began very much like this one had only when Hundley rose before dawn and scaled Sugar Mt. all those years ago Garrett had come with him. Garrett and he were never what you would call friends but they had been sort of attached by fate their entire lives. They grew up in the same town, went to school together and eventually were sent to war together. And in truth, no matter what Garrett thought, after he'd saved Hundley's life Hundley did feel like he owed the man something. So he thought he'd take him hunting. The peace and quiet of the woods had always been soothing to Hundley and he thought if he could get Garrett to see that side of the sport it would be kind of like a gift to him.

So they made their way up to this very tree stand

and took their seats. Like most days hunting they spent a great deal of their time seeing nothing in the way of a deer. All hunters agree that if they were to hunt squirrels, birds or little white butterflies they'd all be raging successes. That is because the majority of the time those things are all you see in the woods. That's how Hundley and Garrett's day went.

Then shortly before sunset as the world was beginning to turn grey and the shadows were lengthening Hundley heard something. Garrett was packing up the gear preparing to head for home when Hundley motioned for him to stop and be quiet for a minute. Garrett obliged and the two men peered into the shadowy woods in silence. Then the unmistakable sound of footsteps came from off among the trees. Garrett tapped Hundley on the shoulder and pointed to the right across the meadow. At first Hundley didn't see it then the buck raised its head and stepped out toward the clearing. Hundley smiled and hooked his thumb at the deer. Garrett looked at him blankly. Hundley pointed at the rifle and again hooked his thumb in the direction of the deer. Garrett caught on but he shook his head and mouthed, "Oh no, you do it."

Hundley whispered, "Are you sure?"

Garrett nodded in the affirmative.

Hundley shrugged his shoulders and picked up his old .30-30, which back then was actually a new .30-30. He leveled the gun and sighted in on the deer. Gently he squeezed the trigger and the silence was shattered in an instant. The explosive report from the rifle echoed across the face of the mountain. The buck leapt and fled off the way it had come and vanished into the woods.

"You missed it," Garrett said.

"I did not. Come on," Hundley said as he led the way out of the tree-stand and down to the ground.

They crossed the field to where the buck had been. There on the frozen ground was a big pool of bright red blood. The blood trailed off across the field along the deer's retreat like a trail of bread crumbs. Hundley punched Garrett in the shoulder smiling widely.

"I told you I didn't miss, hot damn!" He said.

"Well, where is it?" Garrett asked.

"We have to track him. He'll run until he's out of steam. We have to find him fast though, the sun is giving out on us," Hundley said this last as he stole a glance at the rapidly darkening sky. Already it was getting much colder than it had been just a short time before.

So the two men entered the woods though only one

would ever come out again.

Present day Hundley broke the silence and brought them both back from their woolgathering. He grunted more to himself than to Garrett, "Ancient history."

Garrett conceded with a nod, "You're probably right. Besides Ecclesiastes says 'Do not be quickly provoked in spirit for anger resides in the lap of fools.'"

"Yeah, well, when you see Ecclesiastes you tell him he's full of shit. Anger is pretty common among all the folks down here, the smart ones as well as the fools. And speaking of fools; tell him the Tea Party idiots have been cribbing lines from him for years. As if the people in the bible cared a tin shit for American politics."

"That's positively poetic coming from you. See that's the kind of charm and whit that got me out here in the first place. But don't change the subject Hundley."

"Ain't no subject. You're dead. It's been sixty years. Move on."

Garrett would have been surprised by the obtuse attitude Hundley had toward his demise and subsequent fate if he hadn't heard all of this many times before. So he just smiled and ignored the ignorance of his closed minded friend. He would see soon enough.

"Sixty years, a day, forever, it's all the same to me you know," Garrett said.

"Don't know, don't care. All I know is no deer are gonna come anywhere near this tree-stand if you don't quit your yapping."

"Oh, you know they can't hear me you old coot. But they can hear you, right? So, perhaps you should just listen instead of talking for awhile, eh?"

Hundley grunted by way of a reply and continued his surveillance of the field. The sun was rising higher now and a thin fog was rolling up the mountain toward them.

"We both know you've never been the type to think much about the hereafter or about much of anything at all really for that matter." Hundley raised his hand and stuck up his middle finger without ever taking his eyes from the foggy meadow. Garrett smiled and went on, "But I'll tell you this; I may not understand all of the rules but one thing is certain, something larger than us controls it all and whatever It is seems to pay more attention to some people than It does to others."

"So," Hundley grunted.

"So, my monosyllabic friend, I have been coming

to visit you every autumn for over fifty years and believe me when I tell you it hasn't been by choice. Did you ever wonder about why this happens? Did you ever wonder why you keep coming up here every year even though you know I'll be waiting?"

"Maybe I have but what difference does it make why? I come and you're here, the sun's yellow, the sky's blue it's all the same."

"Did you ever think that maybe it's some kind of penance?"

"Bah, that's bullshit. You're dead and someday soon I will be too. When that day comes I'll pay the taxman same as everyone, same as you did unless you're some kind of angel or something."

"I can assure you I'm no angel. I am paying too. We both owe a debt much bigger than we know."

"What the hell are you talking about, Garrett. You aren't making any sense at all. I don't owe nobody shit."

"Do you even remember France? Do you remember any of it at all? Surely some of what happened over there must be rolling around in that dusty old brain of yours."

"You mean the kids."

"I do."

"You can't lay that on us. We were just grunts doing what we were told to do."

"You know that's the same argument the bad guys used over there, right?"

"More ancient history."

"Yeah you might be right, but I'll tell you how I know that this is my penance. You, that's how I know."

"Me? What does that mean?"

"I know that this is my hell because it is you I'm forced to visit instead of her."

Hundley didn't say a word but he didn't have to. His face drained of all color and his eyes went cold as stones. Suddenly he felt as if a fifty pound weight was sitting on his chest.

"I can see by your reaction that you know exactly what I mean. If it were my choice as to whom I got to pay these visits to I'd say that maybe this was heaven. But I don't get to choose so that is how I know. She would be my heaven but instead you are my hell."

Hundley's cheeks were already rosy from the cold and now they grew even redder. Alice. He was talking about Alice. She had been Garrett's girl from the time they were all old enough to have a concept of girlfriends and boyfriends. After school he and Garrett had gone off to war and Alice stayed behind and went to college. They all returned home and a short time after that Alice and Garrett were married. But the ill fated hunting trip came shortly after the honeymoon.

At first Alice hated Hundley. She blamed him and him alone for Garrett's death. But Hundley went out of his way to look out for her in spite of her bitter resentment of him. After many years she softened. She got used to him like people get used to April 15th. But even though she came to accept his remorse in time, Alice never truly forgave him.

Again Hundley just grunted, "Ancient history."

"Maybe to you it is. But how do you think she felt about it all?"

Hundley was growing angry now. This new line of conversation was a topic Garrett had never broached before. Hundley was fighting to keep his hands from shaking and that weight on his chest felt even heavier now. It was as if there was a band around his chest constricting him and making it hard to breathe. "I don't know how she felt. Maybe you can ask her at your next shade convention."

"Oh that's right!" Garrett said feigning a sudden realization. "She's on my side of the curtain now isn't she? I wonder why it is I'm not with her watching some eternal sunset on a cloud over Key West. Why do you think that is? Maybe it has something to do with us bulldozing that little ditch over in the French countryside."

Hundley was caught in such a torrent of emotion that he was completely at a loss for words. His jowls were shaking as he fought to control his emotions and the color was dangerously high in his face.

"But enough about the poor little French kids, how about Alice, Hundley? Did she ever let you come on over for the night? I unfortunately can't leave this God forsaken mountain so I'm kind of cut off from the rumor mill. But after I kicked off did you ever get her to lift the old petticoats for you, huh? That's what you really wanted right? The money and the little secret about the war crimes were enough reason to bump me but Alice was the icing on the cake right? All you had to do was get me out of the way so you could have her. Tell me how'd it work out?"

A sharp pain shot down Hundley's back and arm and beads of sweat formed on his forehead and upper lip. The tightness in his chest had now turned into a deep ache and his breathing was becoming even more labored.

"That ain't what happened at all you delusional specter," Hundley said. The words came hard like trying to yell in a wind storm. It was as if he couldn't get his voice loud enough without a tremendous effort.

"Sure it is. Everyone knew you were sweet on her. So you lured me up here to bump me. Tell me what would have happened if you hadn't shot that deer? If that old buck hadn't made your job easier by leading us out into the woods what would you have done? Would you have used your 'pepper mill' on me?"

"You're crazy."

Garrett went on, "But you didn't have to. You didn't have to kill me in cold blood. Fate bailed you out again. Come on Hundley you know the story."

"Not my fault. It was an accident," he grunted.

"Sure, sure," Garrett said as he gazed out on the meadow. Then he went on in a reminiscent tone. "We walked around in those woods for hours looking for that damn deer. The sun went down and we completely lost the trail. It was freezing. Then you decided we should split up to find it. Split up! I was a lifelong townie. I'd never been more than fifty feet into these woods in my life."

"Oh come on Garrett. You were a soldier. You just said yourself how much of a hero you were in the French woods. Don't blame me because you were inept out here," his voice was little more than a wheeze now.

Garrett ignored him, "By the time I froze to death four days later I was in so much pain I no longer cared that I was starving."

"Not my fault."

But Garrett was on a roll. "Tell me buddy, was she worth it? Was she good in the sack? I always liked it but pussy is kind of like steak; everybody has their own opinion. How'd you like hers?"

Now the pain shot through him like a knife and he grabbed his chest. "Never… touched her… tried to… help her…protected…"

Garrett still ignored him. He looked out at the meadow. The sun was fully awake now. The fog had burned off and a few chickadees were noisily flitting around in the brush. The morning light illuminated

Hundley's startling new complexion in ghastly detail. Beads of sweat stood on his waxy skin in spite of the cool air. But Garrett didn't care. He knew the truth that Hundley had yet to see.

"In truth I hope you did nail her because I have to tell you, if I really died over a God damned deer I'd be pretty pissed off." Then he glanced at Hundley and said, "Hey pal, are you feeling okay? You don't look so hot?"

Hundley dropped the rifle and it clattered to the floor. The man himself slumped against the old maple tree in obvious agony. Garrett savored the moment. Serves the old fool right, he thought to himself. He was still amazed that Hundley was too blind to see the truth and the simple key to relieving his torment. One more little nudge might be enough.

"Please," Hundley gasped. "Help me."

"Oh, now this seems familiar to me," Garrett said. "Where have I seen this before?"

"Please Garrett; I looked after her the best I could. I never betrayed you. It was an accident."

Garrett decided to take pity on him and lead the horse to water. But this would have to be the last straw. If Hundley still couldn't see after this there would be no hope.

"I ask again, did you ever think you old fool, that you have been drawn out here all these years for a reason? Because maybe there is something that God wants you to do. Perhaps this is a gift, Hundley, God's way of letting you do your penance now so you don't have to do a much harder one later. Think, man!"

Hundley looked at him queerly. He was trying to use his rapidly fading mind to make sense of all of this but the business of agony was using most of his resources. What the hell was Garrett talking about?

"You have very little time left Hundley. Better think."

"Garrett it was an accident. I did my best to make it right with Alice.'

"Come on Hundley, that's the same old song, my friend. You can do better."

Hundley stared blankly at him. The agony on his face was palpable. He looked like a drowning man who was gazing at a shore too far away to reach.

"Tell me, Hundley, when was the last time you even saw a deer up here?"

Something in that question triggered a long dormant synapse somewhere in the recesses of Hundley's mind and for a moment he forgot everything else. The heart attack, the ghostly visitor, all of it faded as he considered that question. When was the last time? And why was that question so significant? The answer was right there just beyond his reach. It tormented him like an itch you can't reach. Why did that matter?

Garrett was no help. Hundley looked in his eyes longingly and Garrett remained silent. He just stared back, waiting, eternally patient because eternity is what he had.

Then Hundley said the only thing there was left to say, "Garrett, I'm sorry. I'm sorry to those kids, to Alice, to you…"

After that he rested his head against the tree and closed his eyes.

"There," Garrett said. "Was that so hard?"

Then like the sun coming out after a rain storm, all of Hundley's pain subsided; the pain in his chest as well as that nagging pain of old age. It simply dissipated like steam and he felt like a twenty year old kid.

"What is this?" He asked.

Garrett only shrugged. His face was lit by an odd

little smirk. "I have no idea. But it ain't hell."

Hundley looked at his surroundings completely perplexed. He was looking for understanding but what was happening offered no understanding it simply *was.*

"What happens now?" He asked after a moment.

Again Garrett simply shrugged by way of an answer.

The two sat in the tree stand and looked out on the morning together. Some time later an old grey buck strolled out into the field. It walked up to the pear tree and began nibbling at the little pile of corn. It paused from its feast for a moment and raised its head to look at the big tree at the far end of the meadow. The old wooden stand among the branches was empty as it had been for many seasons now. The deer paid it no mind. He just lowered his head and continued eating the corn as a tiny drone bee zipped past him and landed on a branch of the pear tree.

Jason R. LaPoint
November 18-20, 2013
Johnstown, Queensbury, Thurman and Saratoga Springs, NY

Last Goodbye

"A bird doesn't sing because it has an answer it sings because it has a song."
-Maya Angelou

Part 1- Friday Night

It had been raining for a week straight. A few times it let up but it never completely stopped, there had been at least a light mist in the air the entire time. But that is fall in the Adirondacks. The leaves just start to turn into what promises to be an explosion of color and then a week of rain comes along and ruins the whole works. So it was a pleasant surprise to step out the door of the hospital on Friday evening to find a clear starry sky. Good deal, I thought as I took a deep breath of brisk fall air and headed across the parking lot.

I had been pulling extra long shifts all week but now thankfully the week was over. Friday evening is a rapturous experience after a week of working too long and too hard especially at a hospital. The television shows would have you believe it is a dramatic and heroic place to earn your bread. According to Hollywood everyone in a hospital is a doctor or a nurse and we all save lives every shift and have some life altering revelation each day that enriches our lives and the lives of those around us. In truth the majority of the people who work in these places are peons like me. We are people who do the bidding of the doctors and nurses and instead of saving lives we are really doing little more than either placating people who are perfectly healthy or trying in vain to comfort those who are anything but. In prime time doctors take x-rays and nurses draw blood but in the real world that's not how it works. In the real world there is an army of unsung workers who wade through blood and puke and wipe up crap because there isn't a doctor alive who would do that part. We dry the tears of our patients, their families and often ourselves and coworkers when the pain and the stress get a little too real. We do it everyday for the simple reason that someone has to. We are the people who keep a hospital running and you will never see a prime time drama about any of us.

I had been at work since six that morning, twelve long hours, which was sufficiently long enough for me to forget where I'd parked my car. When I got to the employee lot I started playing the key-fob-hide-and-seek-game. Thankfully I didn't have to play for long. After searching just a few rows the lights of my old Nissan blinked and the horn chirped enthusiastically.

I got in and cranked the car over. I was greeted by the wipers and the stereo both of which I had left on that morning in my haste to get to work on time. I shut off the wipers and turned up the radio. Jeff Buckley was just setting sail on Mojo Pin with that silky voice of his. If there is anything better to hear immediately after getting out of work than him I don't know what it is.

I guided the car out of the lot onto Park Street and headed toward downtown Arkham Falls. The city isn't a hub of culture but it isn't a ghost town either. It's like any other middle class, middle-American town I guess. It's a collection of ten thousand or so hard-working people of all different ilks and persuasions. Many of them are from families who have been in the city since its inception back in the late 1700's. They are mill workers, craftspeople and trade workers like me. Arkham Falls is true blue America through and through. On a Friday night there are a several places downtown where they can go to cut loose with some like minded folks.

I cruised past Wallabies Jazz Bar on Market Street and smiled as the sax music wafted out on the wind and mixed for a moment with Jeff's melody. The streets were starting to give themselves over to the night. The lights were coming on and they shimmered in the puddles and on the shiny skins of the passing cars. The banks, insurance offices and barber shops were going dark and the neon lights of the pizza joints and the bars were coming on as the first of the night's patrons started to emerge from their daytime lives. You can't say this town has got no heart; you just got to poke around.

I pulled into the parking lot of Justice Wine and Liquor and drove around back. A strange sense of déjà vu came over me as I walked in the back door of the store. I went in through the back door for the soul reason that the box wine is kept right inside of it. The "cardboard-deaux" is my favorite selection and it's all I drink. I once had a wine expert tell me that the finest wine is the one that you actually like. I couldn't agree more and what I like is a nice Merlot out of a cardboard box. That's just the way it is.

The bell over the door rang when I went in like it always did. I grabbed a box of wine from the stack without even looking and then made my way to the front of the store.

Martha was on tonight. Martha Adams had been one of the clerks at Justice since I used to come in with my old man when I was just a ten year old kid. She always had a smile and a lollipop for me whenever we came in. Now the lollipop was gone but the same old smile always lit her face whenever I came in and plunked my box of vino on the counter. Tonight the smile looked different somehow. I don't know if it's because I was tired from work or what, but for whatever reason I didn't really notice it at the time. But looking back now it is clear as a bell; her smile was... off.

I slid a twenty across the counter and didn't wait for change which was something I had picked up from dad. Tipping shouldn't be reserved only for waitresses and barbers. Any good job should be rewarded if you are able to do so. My dad believes that and so do I. I told

Martha she was beautiful like I always did and took my wine and left.

I stowed the wine in the backseat then I got in and fired the car up again. Jeff was just starting that cool slide guitar intro to Last Goodbye as I pulled out onto Aviation Road and headed for home. The light changed at the big intersection and I stopped to wait. I sat at the stoplight trying to sing along and failing miserably. As I warbled along to the radio I watched the other cars zip by heading to their respective destinations. Sometimes I wonder where all these people are going. But not that night, all I was thinking about right then was where I was going, which was home, sweet home.

The light turned green. I looked perfunctorily to my left at the oncoming traffic. Then I pulled out onto Route 9 and headed up Miller Hill toward home as I sang along to Last Goodbye.

Part 2- Surprise!

I love my house and it was love at first sight. It was a brilliantly sunny but frigid morning in February twenty years ago when our realtor, Mary Sullivan, brought my wife Kate and I to see it for the first time. I knew as soon as I got out of the car that this would be the home Kate and I would raise our family in and from the look on her face she did too. We did the required tour and the required haggling over the price and the required looking at other houses. But in truth our decision had already been made right there in the driveway on day one.

It is a cream colored cape with brickwork that rises up to just below the windows on the first floor. We have done some landscaping here and there to make it our own but other than that it stands pretty much exactly as it did when we first saw it. All we ever thought the house really needed was a loving family to call it home.

That night as always coming home felt like heaven. But, immediately I noticed something was odd about the house. Every light was on and it was getting late. The girls should have been getting ready for bed by now. For a split second I wondered if something was wrong then it dawned on me what was going on. You know you are either working too much, getting old or both when you actually forget your own birthday.

I was smiling to myself as I grabbed the wine out of the backseat and started up the walk. I noticed that the ashtray was out on the porch. That could only mean one thing; my mom was here. Both Kate and I quit smoking when the damned things got up to five bucks a pack. Now days the ashtray stayed tucked away in the junk drawer in the kitchen with the few remaining butane lighters we still had kicking around. The only time it was ever taken out was when my mother visited. Although the family was constantly at her to quit she was just too stubborn to take the leap unless it was on her own terms, which apparently had yet to be negotiated.

Even though I knew what awaited me when I opened the door I decided to put on my best surprised face out of respect for Kate and her noble attempt at getting one past me.

I opened the door and tossed my keys on the little table in the foyer. I called out, "hello," to which no answer came. Then I entered the living room and the need to feign surprise vanished. I was truly shocked at how many people were there. Kate had managed to organize the least organizable group of people in the world. Nearly my entire extended family and every real friend in my life from the last fifteen years or so was there. To top off the feat was the fact that they all fit into our humble little house in relative comfort.

"Surprise!" They yelled.

I had to admit I was surprised and also very touched. This was the single most loving thing that anyone had ever done for me.

Out of the group came my two daughters. I knelt down and hugged them both at once. There is no feeling quite like a hug from your kids. The warmth of their touch, the smell of their hair, it is the madness of love that drives us on.

"Happy Birf-day Dada," Emma said. Not too shabby for a two year old.

Aubrey said, "Happy Birthday Dad."

Aubrey is a beautiful and bright girl. She is fifteen and at the age where she's not really comfortable acting like a kid but she's also not quite ready to stop acting like one either. She has recently taken to calling me dad rather than daddy, that is unless she is hurt or scared, she wants something or she is in trouble. She's trying to find her way and keep her dignity while doing so, just like everyone else in the world. She's just too young to realize yet that this particular struggle never ends.

Emma is what you might call an "oops kid". She is our little happy accident. Neither of us was really planning on having a baby on our twentieth wedding anniversary but two years ago that's just what we did. But we have never looked back from the moment Kate came out of the bathroom that morning with a look of shock on her face and two pink strips on the pregnancy test. Emma is a doll and she has been an absolute blessing in our lives. And though she rarely admits it the baby has been a source of joy for Aubrey too. It was an adjustment having a new baby in the house just as she was becoming a teenager but adjust she did. Now the two of them are like peanut butter and jelly; separable but better together.

I was moved almost to tears as I thanked them and hugged them tightly. Then I tickled Emma's ribs and she pulled away squirming and giggling. I looked up from the girls to see Kate standing behind them waiting her turn.

I stood up and gave her a tender kiss and then

hugged her too.

"Happy Birthday," she whispered.

"Thank you so much. You have no idea what this means to me," I said.

"Oh, I think I do," she said. Then she took me by the hand and we turned to face our guests. She presented me with a Vanna White-like flourish to the group which got her a few chuckles.

From then on a stream of hand-shakes, hugs and cheek kisses went on for a long time. All the while I kept coming back to how amazing it was to see them all together. I simply couldn't imagine how much work Kate had put into pulling this off. But one thing was certain; I loved her with all of my heart for doing it.

Part 3- Dad

After the initial greetings were through and some brief catching up was done people started mingling. Conversations that were in progress before I had arrived resumed and new ones were started. I made my way over to the dining room table which was packed with food. All of the usual hits were there; Kate's mother's bread dip, Aunt Cecelia's macaroni salad with the fresh basil in it, Mom's orange surprise, the surprise she says is that there is no orange in it at all, and of course Kate's contribution; home made hot wings. There were two things that made me fall in love with Kate in the first place. One was that she loved good music. The second was that she loved cooking finger food and watching sports. Her wings were by far her best creation in that department.

I was glad to see everyone but I was also starving. I hadn't had a bite to eat since eleven that morning and the aromas coming from the dining room had me delirious. I had devoured two wings and was just about to attack a third when I felt a familiar hand on my shoulder. I turned around and looked into the eyes of my father. It was impossible to miss the tears he was barely holding back even as he smiled.

My old man was just twenty two years old when I was born. When I was growing up he had an awful temper that bordered on a mean streak. More than once I went to school with a shiner or a puffed lip at his hand. He had a hard time keeping jobs when I was a kid. He also had a hard time dealing with being a father at such a young age. It's tough having a kid when you aren't really done being a kid yet yourself. It's an old story that has been going on since stories have been going on. To make matters worse I was a bit of a challenge as a kid too. I didn't exactly make it easy on him. More times than I can remember a call from the principal would beat me home and Dad would be waiting for me in the doorway when I got there, red in the face and spitting nails.

But over time he learned to accept who I was and who he was and what he needed to do. He learned that you don't have to live up to anybody's expectations in life but your own. He took control of his life and helped steer me in the direction I needed to go to keep myself out of real trouble. As I grew up I watched him evolve into a good man, a strong man. The relatively small gap in our ages actually helped us grow closer as I got older. As I matured I was able to understand him better. And he was young enough to remember living through most of the trials I was going through myself as a young father and husband. Now I can honestly say he's more like a friend than a parent to me. But it wasn't always that way. We had a rocky road getting to where we are today but in a way I'm glad for it all. There is a reason for everything.

"Getting soft on me big guy?" I said with a grin.

"Happy Birthday son," he said. His tone was somber.

"What is it Dad?"

He looked down at his shoes for a long moment then he drew a breath and looked back to my eyes. Then he said, "I don't think I've made you understand just how proud of you I am boy."

"Dad…," I started, but he waved me off and went on.

"No listen for a minute. All of my errors are made right in you. You have grown into a good man and a great father. I watch you, the way you are with those girls and with Kate and I see how much of a fool I was. You are what I wish I had been. I just never knew how to do it like you do. Can you understand what I mean?"

I stood there dumbfounded with orange stained fingers fighting the urge to well up. I hadn't even recovered from the surprise of seeing all these people and here was the old man throwing me a ball completely out of left field. I definitely wasn't prepared for this. I nodded back at him; it was all I could do. I could only imagine how hard it must be for him to say this to me. He wasn't as bad a man as he thought, though he did leave proof of his anger on my mother and me several times while I was growing up. But to hear him speak so frankly about it, for him to show such honest remorse made me very proud of him. It was a testament to how far he had come.

"Son you have no idea how sorry I am that I laid my hands on you and your mother like that. But the mistakes I made as a young man have turned into blessings now that I'm an old one. Both you and your mother are still in my life, many men like me don't have that luxury. The love and forgiveness you both have shown me has given me the strength to forgive myself and that is the hardest thing in life to do. I just wanted you to know how I feel."

With that he looked back at his shoes. I didn't

know what to say, so I just hugged him. There was nothing I could add, there was no response I could give. I was surprised and overwhelmed with respect. Most people make a few big mistakes in their lives but it takes true courage to own them and try to atone, and it takes even more courage to talk so openly about those mistakes to another person.

After a few minutes we started picking at the food. Then he said something about his new boat and Mom's cataract surgery and before long we were having far more typical conversation. We talked about fishing and the Jets and soon we were right in step with normal life again. But that conversation is one that I will cherish for all eternity. It is when my dad became my hero.

Part 4- Ted Kimble

The first time I met Ted Kimble I was thirteen years old. It was the first day of modified baseball tryouts. My nerves were already pressed to the limit because of the tryouts. The last thing I needed was some pecker-head starting trouble with me, but that's just what he did.

Being a Boston Red Sox fan brings with it an inherent level of misery. On top of that those of us who live in New York have to endure constant heckling from Yankee fans. It's something you find out at a young age and just sort of come to live with in time. I never gave it a second thought that morning as I tossed on my blue hat with the big red B on the front and headed to the baseball field.

That walk was a long one. It was a muggy morning and even though it was only seven o'clock the sun was already beating down. But it could have been a blizzard and I wouldn't have noticed. I was so nervous nothing would have distracted me from my thoughts.

I had never played against kids that were older

than me and I never had to try out for anything before. Add to that the fact that the baseball field was at the high school. The school was an edifice of impending doom that would be looming over me the entire day. The transition from middle school to high school was still months away but if I told you it wasn't weighing on me already even then, I'd be lying.

I had no more than stepped through the gate and onto the field when Ted started in on me. He walked up to me on the outfield grass and shoved my shoulder.

"Hey, what's the B on your hat stand for? Is it baaaaby?"

Some of the kids who were close enough to hear him chuckled and then went on playing toss and fielding grounders. Ted smiled proudly.

"No it stands for back off," it was the best comeback I could muster at the time.

I started to push past him. But Ted, not wanting me to show him up, stuck out his foot and shoved me to the ground. Back then Ted was a lot bigger than me; taller by a foot and at least twenty pounds heavier. But that didn't stop me from jumping up and tackling him to the ground. We grappled on the ground as the other players ran over to us. Ted quickly got the advantage and started punching me in the kidneys until finally some of the older boys dragged him off me and broke us up.

The coach rushed over and yelled something at both of us. I really couldn't hear anything he was saying right at that moment. The red hot rage pulsing through my head had all of my attention. I stood up and dusted myself off. Then I retrieved my glove and my lucky Sox hat.

As everyone else dispersed the coach looked at me and said, "Are you alright? He really put a pounding on you."

I just looked at him and said, "Yeah, I'm okay, where do you want me?"

He looked at me for a second with a little smirk on his face and then he chuckled. He said, "Come on, I have just the spot for a kid like you."

He led me over to where the pitchers and catchers were working out. He handed me a catchers mitt and helped me put on the gear. He said any kid with grit like that was a born backstop that even Munson would be proud of. I ignored the Yankee reference and got to work.

Ted apologized to me later for the fight. He said it

was because he was a new kid to our school and he was just trying to show off a bit so the bigger kids wouldn't ride him. I was just lucky enough to be the next person who came along. There was no harm done. After coach broke up the fight I became a star catcher who made varsity in my freshman year and Ted rode the pine for two years until he finally quit baseball altogether. I was a minor legend on the baseball field for four years which got me all sorts of perks in school and around town. It also got me laid more times than I can count. So his apology was accepted.

  From that point on we actually became pretty good friends. Throughout high school we hung out all the time. That's how Ted met my sister Holly. Girls are always a priority for teenaged guys. Spending time chasing them and spending time with them are pretty common pass-times. Unfortunately beating the crap out of a friend who tries to take advantage of your kid sister in the back seat of a Honda Civic is also a fairly common occurrence.

  Holly was Ted's date to the spring formal in our senior year. After the dance they went out for pizza and then on the way home Ted took the common detour that anyone who grew up in Arkham Falls is familiar with; the canal locks. The locks are a defunct part of the canal system that used to run through Arkham Falls back when it was still a booming timber town. Now the locks are just a cool spot for high school kids to go parking and smoke weed.

The next morning when Holly came down for breakfast with a bruise on her cheek she told mom she fell at the dance. Later I asked her what really happened. Reluctantly she told me that Ted brought her to the locks, they were making out and he wanted more than she was willing to give. He didn't rape her but he did rough her up. When she finished the story I was boiling mad, but she begged me not to do anything. She said it was just the heat of the moment and that Ted really was a good guy. So, out of respect for Holly I didn't do anything; that is until Monday morning.

By the time we got to school I just couldn't hold it in any longer. I caught up with Ted amid the throng of kids as they were herding through the front doors of the school. I grabbed him by the shoulder and spun him around. I could tell from the look in his eyes that he knew exactly what this was about.

"So you like hitting girls do you? Why don't you try hitting me asshole?"

A fight circle instantly formed around us. The hushed group of students was anticipating the action. There is no better way to start a school week than with a good fight. Ted tried to back away but the circle didn't allow it. I dove at him and knocked him to the ground. I got off three good punches to his face before the cheering started. I had him lathered up pretty well by the time the principal finally burst through and pulled me off him.

"Alright that's enough, break it up," he said as he held me at bay.

"He started it Mr. Hudson," Ted whimpered through his bloody front teeth.

"I don't care who started it, I'm ending it and you're both coming with me.

In Hudson's office we each took turns explaining our side of the story. In the end we both got detention. I expected my father to be waiting for me when I got home that night and he was. But this time he didn't hit me or even yell at me. He took me into the garage and we talked about a fishing trip he had been planning to take me on. He didn't say he approved of me fighting to defend Holly but he made it pretty clear that he did. It was one of the first bridges he and I crossed together.

To get back at me Ted started flirting with my girlfriend Allison. It was only about two weeks later that I caught them together. Ted was having a party at his parents' camp in Cleverdale. I got there a little late and I found the two of them making out in the boathouse. I think the only reason he invited me to the party was so that I could catch them. I was mad of course but I got over it pretty quickly. I'd only been dating Allison for a few weeks anyway and honestly I found her droll and a little dumb. In hindsight it was probably for the best. About three months later I heard that Ted's folks had to bring him to the doctor to begin anti-viral treatment for herpes so I consider that a win anyway. Allison gave him the gift that keeps on giving and she gave me the freedom to go to college single, which in turn allowed me to meet Kate.

In spite of all our troubled history Ted and I ended up being friends in adulthood. When I graduated college I had some trouble finding a job in my field so I took a position at a garage in town for awhile. I was no mechanic but dad knew Al Quinn Sr. the guy who owned the place and talked him into letting me run errands and keep the shop clean until I could get on my feet. One night near closing I was sweeping up and Ted came in to drop his car off to have some work done. We started talking and come to find out the four years that I'd spent in college Ted had spent in the Marine Corps. The change in him was striking. Ted always had a funny habit of not looking directly at you when you were engaged in a conversation with him. It was as if he was always afraid of something. He was skittish like a whipped puppy. All of that was gone now. We decided to go out for a beer the next week. We shot the breeze for hours, reminiscing and catching up on the news about our former classmates and Arkham life in general. I won't tell you he was a brand new man or anything but he was a better one and over time we grew to become good friends. Isn't it funny how some times an enemy who sticks around long enough ends up becoming a friend in time?

As we took the awkward stroll through our twenties Ted and I continued to have differences but like everything else they became more sophisticated as we matured. Our rivalry turned from silly teenage conflicts into something of a personal challenge whereby over time we actually drove each other to professional and personal success. When Ted started his real estate business I had to try to start an insurance firm. My brief insurance career failed miserably but it drove me into healthcare where I have done pretty well for a peon. When Ted found out I was engaged to Kate he proposed to his girlfriend Cindy. Cindy laughed at him and moved away to Texas the next week, thereby giving him his answer in striking fashion.

Sometimes we won, sometimes we lost but through it all we were each other's measuring stick in a way. It has always been an odd relationship but it has been one I have valued nonetheless. And value is what matters in the long run.

Ted had a funny look on his face as he walked across the room. I knew he was going to make some kind of speech. It must have been the night for it. My birthday seemed to have turned them all into Hallmark card writers. Sentimentality from my dad was one thing, but from Ted it would just be weird.

But I'd read him wrong. Ted came over and shook my hand and simply said, "Happy birthday loser."

Then he smirked and stood beside me silently. The two of us stood and took in the scene for a long time. We watched everyone eat and visit. The soft din of conversation was broken by the occasional burst of laughter. Somehow in saying nothing Ted said so much. Sometimes the best way to connect to a person is through silent companionship. I knew what Ted felt and he knew what I felt. It was equal parts disdain and respect. It was not a buddy movie kind of friendship. It was a real one. We had been each others shoulders to cry on and we had also exchanged punches several times. Most importantly we had also forgiven each other's trespasses several times and here we were. Our grass-stained knees had been replaced with khaki slacks. We had salt and pepper hair and crows feet where flat-tops and Wayfarers had once been. Childhood trials had turned into mid-life crises. But we were here and that meant something.

Part 5 - Kate

I met Kate when we were both in college at Whittier University here in Arkham Falls. There is a little bar and grill called the Naked Turtle on the shore of Lake Simone. It is downtown in that hip little lake shore section that the city planners dreamed up back in the 1970's. The area is dominated by trendy bars, book stores and coffee shops with a few retail stores mixed in for good measure. It is all connected by a wide sidewalk that runs along the shore. The sidewalk has pictures of the various species of fish that can be found in the lake stamped into the concrete. This area known as College Mile is within walking distance of the Whittier campus and just like the planners intended it is very popular among the students at the school. What good little sheep they train us to be in these institutes of higher learning; Capitalism at its finest.

One evening after a grueling day of classes I needed a break so I headed down to the Turtle for a plate of steamers and a pint of the cheapest draft beer I could find.

The sun was setting over the lake. It was the time of day when the Turtle crowd was just starting to change over from families having dinner to wound up college kids looking to blow off steam at the bar. It was too early to start acting crazy but it was late enough to begin thinking about it.

I took a seat at the bar overlooking the back patio. The Turtle has this great patio that is right out over the water and there is no better place in Arkham Falls to watch the day slip away.

The bartender was named J.T. He was a Whittier dropout from probably a decade or so before. He was older than most of the students but not so much older that he didn't fit in with our crowd. He was a real hipster with a six inch high lime-green Mohawk hair cut. He always wore a Reservoir Dogs style suit to work and claimed to be a Rastafarian. He was never without a story about the school and the stories invariably turned into some dissident opinion on higher learning in general. He was a real colorful character and all the students who loved the Turtle also loved J.T.

J.T. came over and asked me what I needed.

"A plate of steamers and a pint of oat soda, brother," I said.

He snapped his fingers and fired a finger pistol at me then disappeared to the kitchen to place my food order.

While I waited I looked out at the lake. The view was awesome, it was one of the ones that made this place famous in the first place. My moment savoring the sunset was interrupted by a group of girls who were out on the patio. They were chatting and giggling intermittently. Like every guy that age I was usually a walking hormone time-bomb but honestly at that moment I cared a lot less about the fact that they were a group of girls than I did about the fact that they were interrupting my reverie. But it was a bar so I just accepted it and looked them over.

At first glance it was nothing to report, just a group of Whit Twits as we called them. They were a group of four twenty-something girls who were dressed in the usual college girl fashions. They were giggling and drinking a pitcher of beer while they perused the Turtle menu. There was nothing at all to about them that was different from the ten other similar groups of Whit Twits all around the place.

J.T. brought me my beer and plunked it down in front of me. "Scenery doesn't exactly suck tonight, right mon?"

I nodded and sipped the beer.

"You're steamers soon come, okay."

"Okay, J.T. Thank you," I said.

Again he gunned me down with the finger pistol and went off to wait on a group of guys who had just come in.

There was a DJ setting up a karaoke system in the dance hall. He kept testing his speakers with various college bar standards like AC-DC, Steve Miller and Escape Club; all of the bands he played were like the J.S. Bach of the early nineties. The first thing Kate did that made me notice her had to do with the music.

The Smiths, "How Soon is Now" ended and there was a moment of silence from the PA. The sounds of the bar filled the void; clinking glass and the din of twenty simultaneous conversations punctuated by the occasional burst of laughter. Those sounds are there all the time underneath the music but you never really hear them, even though you do. Out of these bar sounds emerged the mellow walking guitar lick from "Summertime" by Sam

Cooke. It has always been one of my favorite songs. But it seemed completely out of place compared with what the DJ had played so far. I found out later that the other songs were just sound checks and that Sam Cooke was much more indicative of the type of music this guy usually spun. That is until a karaoke victim would come along forcing him to revert to more modern selections. It was just one of those quirky-cool things about the Turtle and College Mile. The atmosphere was always just a little bit off from what you might expect. A lot of kids dug it. I certainly did.

Most of the people in the bar paid the music no mind anyway. I watched them as I ate my clams. Everyone was smiling, talking and generally having a good time. I looked back out at the group of girls on the patio and was somewhat surprised to see one of them singing along to herself with Sam as her friends prattled on. Somehow seeing her like that, doing her own thing without her friends even noticing, even though they were right there with her, made her seem very interesting. I have always felt like an observer in the world, like all of this is some kind of stream and I'm a pebble stuck on the bottom as all of it flows around me. In that moment Kate looked something like that too. The life inside the Turtle was going on all around her and she was part of it and not a part of it simultaneously. She was having a private moment in a public setting. I thought she was the most beautiful thing I'd ever seen.

Her back was to the lake. She was perched on one of those high top stools with her legs crossed, one foot hooked around the leg of the chair. Her body swayed very slightly to the music. Her head was down and her eyes were closed as she sang to herself. "Your daddy's rich and your ma is good looking…" She had a straight dark hair that framed her face. I watched her in awe.

When the song ended she opened her eyes and looked up slowly and her eyes met mine across the void between us. I hadn't realized I was staring at her until then and I was embarrassed immediately. I dropped my eyes to my beer and tried not to look as supremely stupid as I felt. After a moment I stole a glance back at her and to my surprise she was still looking at me. She picked up her drink and took a sip then looked back at me and smiled. Then she went back to talking with the others. But the moment had happened. We had connected. Neither of us would have ever believed at the time just what that song that moment and that look would ignite. You hear about the magic moment and love at first sight in poetry and song so often that it has become cliché. But believe me my friends it can happen.

Some time later I saw her get up and put on her coat. The four girls were heading out. On their way to the door they walked past me. Kate went by last and when she did she tapped my shoulder and handed me a folded napkin. Then she smiled again and left without a word. When she looked at me with her steel grey eyes and handed me the note I felt momentarily like the hero in some old movie. I unfolded the napkin it simply said "Kate". There was no phone number, no dorm room, nothing, just her name. The game was afoot. I liked her already.

It took me two weeks to find out her last name without appearing like a stalker. I actually spent more effort on the latter than the former which was foolish on my part because I could have had all I needed in the way of information the night we'd met.

I went back to the Turtle two weeks to the day after she'd given me her name and plunked down at the bar. It was early afternoon and the place was nearly deserted. J.T. asked me what I needed and I asked for a tuna melt and diet coke. He shot me with the finger pistol again and disappeared.

I was moping. I'd had no luck finding her and I hadn't seen her around campus at all. I couldn't sleep, I couldn't concentrate on school. In short she had me at sea. I was smitten completely. I was also sick inside because the thought of giving up had actually occurred to me. Every time I thought of quitting though my mind would replay the image of that long dark lock of hair falling across her chin as she sang to herself, "Fish are jumping and cotton is high…" This mental image felt just like slapping myself in the face.

J.T. came back a few minutes later with my order.

"What's wrong, mon? You look like you dropped you oar ova boord." He asked in his strange fake patois.

"Ahh it's nothing, J.T. Just some girl trouble."

"Is there any otha kind?"

I would have chuckled if I hadn't felt like walking into the lake with a bowling ball necklace. Then J.T. righted the ship.

"Tisn't Katey who's got you wound is it? She a great girl, mon."

I looked up in shock. I said, "Wait, you know Kate?"

"Aye, acourse I know 'er. She in 'ere all da time. Her an' that group of poetesses she run wid."

Poetesses, huh? That was another very interesting tid-bit.

"J.T. this is the most important question I have ever asked in my young life so no bullshit okay. Do you know where I can find her?"

He dropped the patois act completely when he answered, though to this day I don't know why. It was strange but he did it just the same. He said perfectly straight faced, "I thought when she gave you the note that you would just ask me then. It would have saved you some very precious time. Her name is Kate Underwood and she is the editor of the Whittier Quarterly Writer's Journal. Don't waste another minute, Jack. Run over there right now and win her over. Girls like Kate come around far less than once in a lifetime."

His somewhat cryptic comments aside I took it all in and I did as he suggested. I nearly tripped over myself getting out of the Turtle and back to Whittier.

The magazine office is on the far side of campus near the science building. It is in its own one story cinder block structure and most of the time it is dormant. The magazine isn't a regular project it only runs once every three months and a lot of the work is done just before and after editions are published. In the months between issues the office got very little use. But I thought I could at least get someone to tell me where to find Kate if there was anybody there.

As I sprinted from the Turtle to the other side of the vast college it started raining abruptly. Sun showers are the strangest weather phenomenon. The sky was bright with mid day sun but it poured rain on me all the way to my destination. When I got to the office I burst through the door panting and dripping all over the place. I had never been inside the building before and I don't know what I was expecting but it certainly wasn't a large open room with a Christmas tree in the middle of it. It was mid May and the sight had me taken aback.

The air conditioning was on and the cold air had me shivering instantly. I was soaked to the bone; though I was so focused I noticed neither the cold nor my soggy clothing.

The place looked deserted. It was lit only by the light streaming in through the window blinds. Then I heard a voice come from an office off to the left.

"Just a minute Missy, I'll be right out."

I was just about to say that I wasn't Missy when she stepped out of the office. She looked up at me and stopped dead in her tracks. She was clearly surprised as much by the fact that I wasn't who she expected as she was by my condition. A smile slowly spread across her face as she crossed the room to the thermostat on the wall. She never took her eyes away from mine as she went. She turned the a/c off then she stood with her hands on her hips looking at me for a moment.

"Well, look at you. I was beginning to think you weren't coming," she said.

"I'm not great at puzzles," I said. Not one of the all time great first lines, I'll admit but my brain wasn't exactly firing on all cylinders around her yet.

"Well, you solved this one."

"I did."

"One of these mornings you're gonna wake up," she said.

"And you're gonna spread your wings and fly," I said

"Close enough for me. We should really get you

dried off before you catch pneumonia."

And with that began the greatest love I have ever known. We spent most afternoons together from then until graduation. We got to know each others pasts, presents and dreams for the future. We found that while many of our dreams for the future were similar many more were not but even those were interesting enough to explore together.

Three years after college we were married. That day was a whirlwind of hand shaking and flash bulbs. I barely remember it at all. I just remember this radiant angel who kept dancing with me. And I remember thanking God over and over again for that weird bartender who made it all possible.

We went to a bed and breakfast in Lake Placid for our honeymoon. It was a wonderful week filled with food, romance and some of the coldest temperatures I have ever experienced. But the freezing weather just motivated us to spend our time doing a whole lot of what honeymoons are for. One night as we lay in bed in the darkness, listening to the soft purr of the innkeeper's snore coming through the floorboards, Kate asked me if I thought this was destiny. I thought for a moment and said that I had no doubt in my mind that it was. She asked if I thought it would last forever. I rolled over and kissed her softly and said that I would love her for all eternity. I meant it then and I mean it now.

I went into the kitchen to get some more ice for the punch bowl. Kate was standing by the island chopping some strawberries when I came in. She looked up and smiled at me as she continued chopping. The steel grey eyes were now marked by the very beginnings of crow's feet and the dark hair was streaked with fine wisps of silver. All in all she was even more beautiful as a middle aged woman than she had been as a twenty year old girl.

"Oh don't worry about the punchbowl, Jack. Get back out there and entertain your guests. This is as much for them as it is for you, you know."

I smiled and walked around the island to stand behind her. I took the knife from her hand and turned her to me. She looked at me for a moment and then sighed. "I really have to get this fruit out there. The natives will get restless if we don't keep them fed."

I held her tight and kissed her long and soft on the lips. She closed her eyes and purred.

"I love you Katy. More than you'll ever know."

Part 6 - Mom

I followed Kate back into the dining room. She had a fresh fruit bowl and I had a punch bowl half full of ice. I set it down on the table and was refilling it with punch when Mom came over and tugged at my arm.

"Come on, let's walk," she said. "I need a smoke."

I frowned but I obliged her.

Once we were outside she sat down in one of the porch chairs and pulled out her cigarette case. She had her eyes on me but she didn't say anything. I felt like I was twelve years old all over again and she'd just seen my report card. That look said she was building up steam to give me hell about something but I didn't know what. The old man was always up front with his anger. He'd smack the holy shit out of me and all the while he'd be screaming at me about my transgressions. Mom on the other hand had her own style. She was more passive-aggressive. She'd calmly talk to me, cutting me to the soul with every word, making me wish the whole time that she'd just belt me up side the head like Dad would have.

She flicked the lighter; the little flame was very bright on the dimly lit porch. She took a pull and the cigarette glowed to life. I could imagine her lungs making the same faint crackling sound the burning tobacco made as the poisonous smoke poured into them.

Still she said nothing; she just looked at me with unreadable eyes behind a veil of smoke.

Finally I said, "What?"

She exhaled a puff and frowned, and then she looked out across the darkened lawn. "I just don't know how to say it," she said.

This was Classic Mom; build the drama one step at a time. I was frustrated and I rolled my eyes.

Though she wasn't looking and could not possibly have seen me she said, "Don't roll your eyes at me because I love you."

So I said all I could say, "I'm sorry mom, I just don't know what you're talking about. Everyone's having a good time. What could you be glum about?"

"Glum. Huh," she said. Then she returned her gaze to the lawn.

For a minute we stayed like that, me standing by the door watching her sit and smoke in silence. Then she stood up and went past me down the stairs to the walkway. She took a few steps and then turned around.

"Well, come on. I need to walk and I'm not sure how much time we have."

Sure enough I was twelve again after all. I had no idea what she was talking about but I followed her obediently anyway.

We walked down the driveway and out onto the street. The evening sky was still clear as a bell just as it had been when I'd left the hospital earlier. The air was chilly but I felt cozy in spite of it. As we neared the end of the block I saw a long line of cars parked at the rec field on Maple St. That is where my sly and sneaky friends and family had hidden all of the evidence, I thought and smiled.

Mom walked on in silence. In the yellow glow of the street lights she looked older than I'd ever noticed before. It was almost as if she had aged a decade since the evening began. Still she walked along, puffing at her cigarette and looking at the yards and houses along the street as we went. Dad's conversation had been strange but it was eclipsed by this eerie lack of conversation from mom. Then a bell went off inside my head at the thought.

I said, "Mom is something wrong with dad?"

She stopped for a moment and looked in my eyes. Hers were filled with tears. She said, "No you foolish boy."

Then she hugged me tightly and wept into my chest. She was shaking and gasping for breath between sobs. I tried to say something to comfort her but nothing came out.

She pulled away from me. She held me by the hands and said, "Don't worry, Jack. The girls will be fine."

I looked at her puzzled by her strange behavior. I tried to ask what she meant but again nothing came out. A strange sensation came over me. It felt as if an electrical current were thrumming through my body and…

Part 7 – Last Goodbye

No one heard the knock the first time, the party noises drowned it out. But the second time the raps were much louder and Aubrey heard them. She had retreated into her own world long ago. She enjoyed the company but like anything else they didn't hold her attention for long. She had been sitting quietly on the loveseat in the den playing Angry Birds on her iPod for awhile now. The second time the knock at the door came she paused the game and went to the foyer to answer it. Her Dad and Gram had gone out a few minutes ago and she thought maybe they'd accidentally locked themselves out. When she opened the door she was taken aback. She never expected to see her Uncle Gerry standing there in his police uniform.

A smile lit her face as she hugged him and said, "Hey Uncle Gerry, I'm glad you made it."

She pulled away from him and stepped aside to let him in. The smile faded from her face as she saw the grave look on his. He simply said, "Hey kiddo, is your mom around?"

Aubrey nodded. "Yeah she's in the kitchen I'll go get her."

She walked down the hall toward the kitchen stealing uneasy glances back at her uncle every so often. Kids have an uncanny sense about things. Her heart was already preparing her for the blow it was about to receive.

A few minutes later Aubrey and Kate returned to the foyer. Kate was drying her hands on her apron as she came down the hall.

"Gerry, come on in, why are you standing there in the doorway, you weirdo."

"Katy, it's about Jack."

Kate said, "Yeah, it's his party. I told you that. I'm glad you could come by. Now get in here."

"No Katy, you don't understand. Maybe you should come outside on the porch for a minute." He said this as he nodded slightly in Aubrey's direction. Aubrey looked confused but tears were already filling her eyes.

"Gerry what are you talking about," Kate said forcing a smile. "Get in here and grab something to eat. Jack and Darlene just went for a walk. They'll be back any minute."

Gerry tilted his head to the side and looked at his sister questioningly. He said, "Katy, you really should come with me for a minute."

Just then Darlene opened the door and came inside. Jack wasn't with her. She looked at Gerry then she looked at Kate and Aubrey. She nodded and looked Gerry in the eyes solemnly and said, "Maybe you should just tell them. I'll go take care of Emma."

Kate looked at Darlene in utter confusion then she looked at her brother as the first of many tears began streaming down her face.

"Katy, earlier tonight someone robbed Justice Wine and Liquor at gunpoint. As the thief was leaving Jack came into the store through the back door. He startled the gunman and the man shot him."

Katy began balling and shaking her head defiantly. "No, no, no, no," was all she could manage.

"I'm sorry Kate but he didn't make it."

Again she repeated her vow, "No, no, no, no!"

Gerry took a step toward her but she backed away as if he were a stranger. Still she kept repeating, "No, no, no!" over and over again and every time did she said it louder as if the repetition or the volume could make it all go away.

Aubrey fell back against the wall and slid her back down. She crouched on the hallway floor sobbing as her mother continued to deny what she was sure to be true.

"Kate, I saw him myself."

"I SAW HIM MYSELF!" She screamed. Her face was red and streaked with tears. "He's been here all night, Gerry! This is his party."

At the last line she lost steam and began sobbing again. The guests were all gathering around now to see what was going on.

Gerry went to his sister and took her by the shoulders. He hugged her close as she sobbed against him.

"Look, I don't know what happened here tonight. But I wouldn't be here telling you this if I wasn't absolutely sure. I saw him with my own eyes, Kate. Jack is gone. He died at Justice Wine and Liquor at 7:35 this evening. Martha the night clerk saw the whole thing. She said he came in the back like he always did. Only tonight it was just his bad luck to walk in on a robbery in progress. The man shot Jack and burst out the back door.

He stole Jack's car and made it to Queensbury before the Warren County Sheriff caught up with him."

Kate pulled away from him. She had stopped crying and now she looked mad.

"Stole his car you say?"

"Yes, Kate I'm sorry. But we got the guy."

Kate marched down the hall to the front door.

"If he stole Jack's car then why is it sitting right there in the driveway where he parked it when he got home?"

She said this and then threw the door open. But all it revealed was Gerry's cruiser sitting where Jack's Nissan should have been. Kate stood in silence gazing out at the driveway. She put her hand to her lips and began sobbing again.

Everyone in the house was as confused as she was. Everyone that is except Darlene who seemed to know exactly what was going on.

Kate feebly said, "But he came home."

Several people nodded agreement. Aubrey simply cried quietly through it all.

"I'm sorry, folks," Gerry said. "I don't know what

you experienced here tonight but Jack didn't come home."

"Yes he did," Darlene said. She was holding Emma in her arms. The baby girl was mercifully oblivious to the entire situation.

"Dar, I just don't see how that's possible," Gerry said.

"It doesn't matter how it's possible. It happened. Jack came to his party tonight. He came for us, so we could all say our last goodbyes. What happened here tonight is nothing short of a miracle. Tomorrow we will all have to live with the pain of this tragedy but tonight Jack came to comfort those of us that he loves."

No one said a thing after that. What could be said really? In the days that followed what was necessary to do was done, tears were cried and questions were asked, though no answers ever came. Then, in time, life returned to something that felt like normality. But no one who was at the party that night ever forgot Jack's last goodbye.

Jason R LaPoint
Started in Glens Falls sometime in 2003, finished in Thurman 11-25-13

Acknowledgments

Books take a long time to write. This one took an inordinate amount of it. Along the way a great deal has changed in my life. Many people have come and gone. But some have been with me all along. I couldn't have done this without them. My family has been amazing. They have supported me and believed in this admittedly elusive dream of mine all along. Mom and Dad, Jess, the kids, my huge collection of aunts and uncles, my grandparents, my in laws, all of them have played a part in keeping this ship afloat. When one is not a professional writer one must be a professional something else. But he is still a writer. It isn't something you can turn off. But because of the need to do something else with most of my time my art often has to take a back seat, which can lead to a lot of frustration. When the book takes a year, then two, then five, then over a decade to complete it can wear on the ego a bit. Doubt can creep in and start chipping away but these folks have each in their own way helped me many times to combat the doubt and keep the wolves outside the door. Now finally this little collection is done and I owe a lot of it to my people.

Thank you to Mom and Dad, Dan and Lorrie, all of my aunts and uncles, Gram LaPoint, the Cousins, Josh Hamell, Tanya Hamell, Larry Gonyea, Nat Nicholson, Alex Hyatt, Jason Thompson, Charity Anderson, Rob Wood, Jarred Smith, Joe Moran, Chad Saville and to everyone along the way who bought me a beer and listened to some weird story idea or complaint about some nuance of this big nebulous thing called writing. All of you have helped. All of you have left an impression. If there is anyone I forgot to mention I sincerely apologize and I will get you next time. I love you all.

To all of the folks to whom I dedicated stories; I almost included the reasons why I dedicated them to you but I thought they felt too personal to publish. In truth I think you will all find your own reasons in the stories themselves; its better that way anyway.

I would also like to include a special note of thanks to Jess for taking the author photo and to her and Avery for helping me edit the manuscript. Any mistakes that made it through the process are entirely my fault but thanks to my girls there are a quite a few less of them.

Thanks to Shawn Hitchcock for the cover photo. If you are ever in Cape Cod and want to hear some cool live music check out Shawn's band the Coozies. Thanks to all of the other artists who I may have borrowed a line or image from along the way. I hope you all have a good sense of humor.

Last and most importantly thank YOU for reading my stories! Without you this would be a lot less fun.

Jason

Follow Jason on the web at:

Jason R LaPoint Writer on Facebook

And

@JayPlus5 on twitter

Stop by to see what's new, give feedback or just say hi!

Jason R. LaPoint lives and works in the Adirondack Park in upstate New York. He is also the author of the novel, *The Red Bank Incident.* His second novel, *Cardinal Pride* is due to be released in the fall of 2014.

Proof

Made in the USA
Charleston, SC
26 March 2014